CHEERLEADERS®

#16

IN LOVE

CAROL STANLEY

D1102649

SCHOLASTIC INC.
New York Toronto London Auckland Sydney

ISBN 0-590-40048-7

12 11 10 9 8 7 6 5 4 3 2 1   4   6 7 8 9/8 0 1/9

Printed in the U.S.A.   01

CHEERLEADERS

IN LOVE

CHEERLEADERS

For Lian, Jennifer, Becs, and Erin

CHAPTER

Less than a minute was left on the huge clock on the Tarenton High gymnasium wall. The scoreboard next to the clock showed the Tarenton Wolves tied with the Washington Cougars. The tension and excitement in the stands on both sides were so thick they were practically additional elements in the air, like oxygen.

The tension sent a thrill through Mary Ellen Kirkwood. Mary Ellen had been captain of the Tarenton High Varsity Cheerleading Squad since the beginning of the school year. By now she knew instinctively how to pull that tension out of the air and channel it. It was like pulling electricity out of the sky and throwing it into a live cable.

1

She whirled around so fast the red and white pleats of her short skirt blurred into pink. Blue eyes blazing, she said to the other five members of the squad, "Come on! Let's push 'em over the top! Let's tell Washington High they might as well take their ball and go home. Let's do 'Don't Mess.' "

Grabbing their megaphones off the hardwood floor of the court, the six of them sprang into line position and began shouting in unison:

> "Don't mess with the best,
> 'Cause the best don't mess!
> Don't fool with the cool,
> 'Cause the cool don't fool!
> What you see is what you get,
> And you ain't seen nothin' yet!
> Come on Tarenton — let's win!"

At the end of the cheer, all six of them threw themselves up into perfectly synchronized spread-eagle jumps. When they dropped back down, they began doing floor jumps in rapid alternation, like pistons, urging the Tarenton fans into a chant of:

> "Let's win!
> Let's win!
> Let's win!"

and not stopping until Donny Parrish, captain of the Tarenton High Varsity basketball team, granted them their wish, slam-dunking the ball through the hoop just as the final buzzer went off.

The crowd went wild.

Mary Ellen felt like all their energy was coursing through her. She jumped up and down, shaking her crimson and white pompons, hugging the other members of the squad, then the team members as they ran past on their way to the lockers, screaming with the people in the stands until her throat gave out.

Most of the time when Tarenton won, Mary Ellen couldn't talk for a whole day after the game. She was too hoarse from putting everything into her cheering. Her mother would fix her mugs of hot tea and chicken broth and mutter about how shouting cheers didn't seem like a good enough reason to ruin a person's vocal chords, but Mary Ellen didn't pay any attention to this.

She loved cheerleading. And being captain of the Tarenton squad was her dream come true. She knew she was the envy of almost every girl in school: tall, blonde, beautiful, popular. Being a cheerleader was symbolic of all this. It said she was at the peak.

And the peak was where she wanted to stay. Which was why she was planning to leave Tarenton after graduation and go to New York. She was going to become a major fashion model and have Manhattan at her feet, just the way she had Tarenton now.

What she was *not* going to do was stay around town and be poor like her mother, married to a bus driver, always scraping through until payday, clipping coupons, and coming up with a hundred and one ways to fix macaroni and hamburger. Nope. If Mary Ellen was going to do any cooking, it would be on the cook's night off, and she'd put together something with Caviar Helper.

Which meant she was not going to marry Patrick Henley. Which meant that, cute and fun and persuasive as he was, she was not going to ever ever let herself fall in love with Patrick. Patrick did not drive a bus. No, it was much worse than that. He drove the local garbage truck.

No sooner had she run through this sequence of thoughts — her standard why-I'm-not-going-to-fall-in-love-with-Patrick rap — than there he was, leaping across the court with his camera, heading toward her.

Patrick was the official Tarenton High photographer, and covered all the games for the school paper.

"Hey, sweetheart," he said now, doing his Bogart impersonation, turning up his collar and putting an arm over her shoulder and giving her a quick kiss — although Patrick's kisses were never quite quick enough to be just friendly. There was always a fire beneath them that stirred up way too much inside Mary Ellen.

She pulled away from him, trying to break free of the spell he so easily dropped over her.

"What a game, eh?" she said, trying to lighten things up.

4

"Sometimes I can't believe those guys!" he said, shaking his head in appreciation. "Or you guys, either, for that matter. You've got to be the best cheering squad around. It must feel great to have all that power, to be able to get hundreds of people on their feet, cheering in unison."

Mary Ellen blushed a little.

"Oh, I think it's the team that gets them cheering, Patrick. We're just responsible for the unison part. But it is great to be in the nice, long middle of the basketball season. You know, when we've finally got all the cheers down pat and can coast a little."

"Yeah," said Angie Poletti, who had come up and been listening in on the last part of this exchange. Angie was the best cheerleader on the squad. The others teased her about having so much natural enthusiasm that she probably did a double cartwheel just getting out of bed in the morning. Now she linked arms with Mary Ellen. "I'm thinking that finally the two of us might get a free Saturday to go shopping at the mall. Like normal, regular teenage girls."

"Right," Mary Ellen said. "Instead of galley slaves on the ship of Ardith Engborg." They weren't really serious. Although their coach Mrs. Engborg *was* a slave driver, they knew she was the one most responsible for the Tarenton squad being as good as it was.

Still, they'd been having five-day-a-week practices since the beginning of basketball season. All six of them were aching for a little freedom.

And it looked like they were going to get it. That is, it looked like this for one brief minute before Ardith came down out of the stands, taking the bleachers two at a time, waving a piece of paper at them.

"Squad! Squad!"

Six heads turned and looked up. And tried to turn back around. When Ardith called them "squad," it meant she had work in mind. But what could it be now, with the season so far along?

Olivia Evans, the star gymnast on the squad, and Walt Manners, the group's clown, wrapped arms around each other's waists, as if bracing each other for whatever news Ardith was bringing. Olivia and Walt were about as solid a couple as you could find at Tarenton.

Pres Tilford and Nancy Goldstein, the other members of the squad, had each been halfway to their respective locker rooms when Ardith came wailing down upon them. They stopped in their tracks and headed back. By the time Ardith reached all of them, they were standing in a loose semicircle.

"I've got some exciting news here," she said, waving the unfolded letter between her thumb and middle finger. "It looks like cheerleading is finally getting the respect it's due. For the first time ever, there's going to be a tri-state high school cheerleading competition. Squads from all over are invited to come."

"Where is this going to be, Mrs. Engborg?"

6

Olivia asked, already dreading the task of getting her overprotective mother to let her travel out of town. Olivia had undergone heart surgery when she was little, and ever since then her mother acted like she was just out of intensive care.

"Summerville," Ardith said. "I guess because it's centrally located."

"When?" Pres asked. His girl friend Claudia had been after him to take her down to Florida over spring break, a romantic road trip in his Porsche.

"About a month from now," Ardith said. "Over spring break. I hope none of you made any plans for then. I really think we ought to go. I've seen other squads, at our games, and driving around the area on weekends . . ."

The six cheerleaders exchanged looks. Sometimes it was hard to believe Ardith's dedication to cheerleading.

". . . and I really think you've got a chance at winning the tri-state title."

"You really do?" said Mary Ellen.

Ardith nodded seriously, then said, "But you'd really have to gear up. It would mean workouts every day after school — and double workouts on Saturdays."

All six cheerleaders groaned in unison. Ardith threw up her hands.

"Okay, okay, I know I'm asking a lot. More than you signed on for. So if you don't want to do it, I'll understand. It's strictly up to you. Talk about it among yourselves, and let me know one way or another Monday. I have to send them a response."

She walked away without smiling, making it clear that she really wanted them to do this, but knew it had to be their decision. The six of them stood together on the now empty court.

"Let's change and meet in the parking lot," Walt said. "I don't know about you, but I always make better decisions on a full stomach. I say we have a powwow at Pizza Pete's."

CHAPTER

When the cheerleaders got outside to the parking lot, they found it had been snowing all through the game. Big, fat, wet flakes. Three or four inches had fallen, blanketing the ground and making the cars look like sleeping white animals.

Walt and Pres began casually packing snowballs and lobbing them at each other.

Olivia turned to Angie and said, "This is the kind of thing that worries me about boys. I mean, how old does the average guy have to be before he stops looking at snow as material for snowballs?"

"That's why they need us," Angie said. "To help them mature and become civilized human beings."

It was at this precise moment that both Angie

and Olivia got smacked with snowballs. Calmly brushing herself off, Angie continued, "Of course, certain members of the species are beyond the reach of civilization. They only understand retaliation." She bent to scoop up enough snow to make a giant ball of her own.

Which she threw at Walt. Who tossed one at Nancy. Who fired off two — one at Pres, the other at Olivia. Who had made a little lineup of her own ammunition on the fender of Walt's Jeep. She knelt behind this barricade and stuck her head up only long enough to take aim and toss another. Mary Ellen waited until Olivia was distracted, though, and snuck up behind her, getting her with two snowballs aimed squarely at her back.

After ten minutes, they were all exhausted, mostly from laughing, and collapsed on the hoods and trunks of the cars, except for Olivia, who was waving her red and white pompon from behind the Jeep as a sign of surrender.

Coming into Pizza Pete's afterward, the six of them looked pretty bedraggled, their hair damp and messy, their jackets soaked, their cheeks red with cold. Everyone looked up as they entered.

Friday nights after games, Pizza Pete's had to be one of the most crowded restaurants in America. Practically everyone from Tarenton High came by to eat pizza and talk about the game and just generally see what was happening — who was going out with whom, who had broken up. Around Tarenton, you practically needed a scorecard to keep up with the romantic action.

The hottest item of interest at Pete's tonight was Vanessa Barlow and Donny Parrish, who were sitting in a front booth by themselves, talking in low tones over a large pepperoni pizza Vanessa was the daughter of Dr. Barlow, superintendent of the Tarenton school district — a position she enjoyed very much. A position she would have enjoyed even more was being on the cheerleading squad. But she had been cut in tryouts last fall, and ever since had hated the six who *did* make it. And with Vanessa, hate was an active verb. She was always on the lookout for some way to do something rotten to the cheerleaders.

Vanessa and Donny stopped talking and looked up as the cheerleaders brushed past their booth.

"Way to go, Donny," Mary Ellen said, brushing Donny's short hair with her hand.

"Yeah," Pres said, slapping Donny with a jock's handshake, "great game."

"Hey," Walt said, bending over the pizza, "this must be serious romance here. No onions on the pizza."

"Yeah, yeah," Donny said. "Get outa here. Hey, why are you all so wet? I knew cheerleaders worked up a sweat, but this is ridiculous."

"A little snowball fight," Mary Ellen said sheepishly.

"Oh, isn't that cute?" Vanessa said, running a hand through her thick black hair. "You kids

11

sure know how to have fun. Now hurry and go have your pizza so you can run back out and make a snowman."

"We just might do that," Nancy said. Then as the others were walking off, she pinched the fabric of Vanessa's sleeve, and said, "Nice sweater."

The sweater in question was black with a flourescent geometric pattern on the front. Vanessa wasn't sure she was really punk, but was kind of trying out the image. She couldn't tell from how Nancy made the remark if she was being serious or sarcastic, so there was no way to know how to respond to it. Since Nancy was so nice, she had probably meant it sincerely. Still, she *was* a cheerleader and Vanessa hated cheerleaders, so she decided to take the remark as sarcastic.

Luckily for the cheerleaders, a big table in the back was open. They sat down and were so hungry they didn't even bother to give Sally, the waitress, a hard time. Usually they tried to drive her nuts by ordering pizzas with pepperoni and cherries. Or mushrooms and walnuts. Or anchovies and kitchen faucets. Tonight they just ordered one large and one medium Pete's Deluxe. When Sally had walked away, Mary Ellen looked at the rest of them seriously and asked, "So, what are we going to do about this competition?"

"Argh," Pres said. "I'm supposed to take Claudia down to Florida over spring break. She

12

won't be happy about a change in plans."

"I was just kind of looking forward to coasting a little," Walt said. "We've finally got our routines down nice and smooth. I was thinking we'd be cutting back practices — not adding to them!"

"I know," Olivia said. "My mother'll be fit to be tied. What do you think, Nancy?" Olivia turned and blew the paper off her straw at her friend to get her attention.

"Oh," Nancy said flatly. "I guess I don't care much one way or the other." Nancy's boyfriend Ben had died in a mountain-climbing accident a few weeks earlier, and since then she hadn't cared about much of anything. The others were trying to bring her around, but so far, no luck.

The table fell into silence, with everyone thinking about Ben, not wanting to say anything for fear of upsetting Nancy even more. Mary Ellen broke into the gloom.

"You guys," she said, looking each of them, one by one, hard in the eyes. "Come on. Sure it'll mean extra practices, but think of the pay-off. When we win — and notice I said *when*, not *if* — we will be the best in the region. Officially. No room for doubt. Everyone for miles around will know it. All the other squads will have to bow before our undeniable superiority."

"Hmmm," said Pres, smiling his slow smile. "You get me in my soft spot — my ego. I guess I'm just going to have to persuade Claudia that she doesn't really want to be tanning on a warm, sunny beach during break; that she wants to be in

Summerville watching us win the competition."

"You really think we'll win?" Olivia said.

"Absolutely," said Mary Ellen.

"Melon's right," Angie said, referring to Mary Ellen by her nickname. "We've never held back before. We've always gone for it, and we can't stop now!"

"I agree," Walt said. "But I don't think we're going to win purely on enthusiasm. We've got to have a strategy. We're good, but everyone knows all our cheers by now. I just don't see how we're going to impress these judges with stuff we've been using all season. We'll have to put something new together."

"Not only new," Mary Ellen said, her blue eyes lit up with excitement. "New and totally astonishing. Until the moment we come out on that floor at that competition, no one but us and Ardith is going to know one word, one move of those cheers. No one."

The others thought about this, and then nodded. The table was silent in agreement. The only voice responding to Mary Ellen was a quiet one on the other side of the big jukebox to one side of the table. Crouched there, pretending to pick songs, was Vanessa. She smiled to herself and whispered, "Is that right, Mary Ellen? You really think no one's going to find out your stupid cheers? *No one?* You think you can keep them a secret from Vanessa? Think again."

14

CHAPTER

The cheerleaders were getting ready to head back out into the snow, bundling up in jackets and long wool scarves and knit caps — Walt, as usual, thumbing his nose at whatever was stylish, this time by wearing an old World War I leather pilot's cap. As they snaked their way between tables, and out of the restaurant, Pres came up behind Nancy and put a hand gently on her shoulder. She was so deep in thought, though, that she jumped at even this soft touch.

"Sorry," he said, "didn't mean to give you a start. Were you on another planet?"

"Sort of," she said, but didn't offer any more.

"What I wanted was a lift home," he told her. She turned and opened her mouth in mock astonishment.

"Preston Tilford III — *without wheels?!* I don't believe it."

"I let Claudia drive the Porsche the other night. I was trying to teach her to drive a stick shift. She did something mysterious and disastrous to the transmission. It's been in the shop for three days now."

"Well, if you'll accept the humble transportation of my mother's Toyota, of course you can come with me. I couldn't leave anyone as cute as you stranded in the cold."

Nancy and Pres had never been romantically involved. Whatever it was that clicked between two people had just never clicked between them. They were safe from each other's charms, which, in a way, made it easier to be good friends. They could tease and flirt outrageously, with no possibility of misunderstanding.

After saying good-night to the others, they walked down the street to where Nancy had parked. They sat in the cold, damp car while the engine warmed up, billowing steamy smoke out the exhaust pipe. Nancy clicked the radio knob and the Talking Heads came on low.

"Where's Claudia?" she asked. "How come she didn't come to the game tonight?"

"Oh, she's totally uninterested in sports. She used to come to home games, but just to see me."

"She doesn't care about seeing you anymore?" Nancy said. She was only teasing, but from the look on Pres's face, she saw she had hit a sore spot. "Hey, I'm sorry," she rushed on.

16

"It's okay," Press said. "Maybe it's nothing. Maybe relationships aren't meant to stay exciting forever."

"Maybe she's just had enough excitement for one year," Nancy offered. Claudia had just come through delicate, dangerous surgery to remove a bone fragment that had been pressing on her spine.

"Yeah, that's probably all it is," Pres said. "She'll probably snap out of these blahs any day now." He didn't sound like he believed a word he was saying. He looked uncomfortable talking about it, then took a leap into another subject.

"What about you? You okay?" he asked.

She nodded and said, "Pretty okay," and put the car in gear and pulled out into the street.

Pres lived out on Fable Point, a small enclave of mansions across the lake from Tarenton. His father owned Tarenton Fabricators, the biggest manufacturer in the area, and his family was one of the richest in town.

Nancy lived with her parents in a nice house on the town side of the lake. If she turned off the highway at Fable Point, she could drop Pres off and then take the lake road around to her house and be home in five minutes.

Instead she turned off at Hawthorne Hills, a new housing development just outside town. At Hampton Lane, she turned left, then slowed down as she drove past 628. Ben's house. His black Isuzu was still parked in the driveway.

"Why are you doing this?" Pres asked softly,

as if he were talking to someone in a trance.

"I drive by every night," Nancy said. "I'm not sure why. It's like I don't want to break the connection. Even though he's dead and I know that, I don't want to let him slip away. The other night as I was going to sleep, I panicked. I couldn't remember what he looked like. I can't even trust my memory."

"Nancy, pull over here," Pres said when they had turned the corner. She did what he asked. When she'd turned off the ignition, he said, "Ben was a special guy. And he was particularly special to you. And I hear what you're saying about not wanting to let his memory just slide off into nothing. But there's a difference between holding him in a special place in your heart, and acting like he's still around in some real way. Driving by to see his car every night is over-the-line behavior."

"Maybe," Nancy said. "All I know is that I feel better seeing it there every night."

"Yeah, well, what are you going to do when suddenly one night it's not there? What if his folks sell it?"

"I'll deal with that if it happens," she said huffily.

Pres leaned back. He knew more pressure would only make her indignant. When she started the car up again, he turned the radio up and they listened to Billy Joel the rest of the way to his house. When they pulled into his drive, he hopped out.

"Thanks for the lift," he said, starting toward

his house. Suddenly he turned around and walked back to her side of the car. She rolled down the window and looked at him curiously.

"I knew there was something I wanted to talk to you about. I just remembered what it was. My dad's company is sponsoring this gym and swim program for handicapped athletes at the junior college in Hillsborough. I said I'd help out in the gym. They need an assistant swimming coach, though, and since you're the only swimmer I know, I promised my dad I'd ask you."

"Oh, I don't think I have time, what with the extra practices and all."

"It's only on Sunday mornings. I could drive. You'd be back by early afternoon. And it would really be doing a good deed. These handicapped jocks really look forward to the program. And they really need another person in the pool."

"Okay, okay," she said, bending her arm behind her back to show him he was twisting it.

"Does that mean okay, you'll go with me Sunday?"

"Yes. All right. I'll go."

"Great. I really appreciate this, Nance. They really need you."

Before Nancy could change her mind, Pres turned and sprinted up to the massive front doors of his house. He went inside and scouted around for his father. He found him working on some business papers in his study. Pres stuck his head in.

"Hey, do you think you could put Nancy

Goldstein in the handicapped program? In the pool or something?"

His father looked up.

"She wants to help out?"

"Sort of. Really, I want her to help out. She's in a slump since Ben Adamson died. I thought maybe getting her focused on helping someone else might take her mind off him."

"Okay," his father said, closing the folder on his lap. "That was thoughtful of you, Pres."

"Oh, and one more thing," Pres said as he was pulling the door shut on his way out. "I told her I was helping out, too, so could you sign me up as a gymnastics coach or something?"

CHAPTER

On Saturday afternoon in the brightly lit, overheated Tarenton High gym, with snow falling softly outside the high, grated windows, the cheerleading squad began practicing for the tri-state competition.

With megaphones held high, the six of them faced an imaginary crowd in the empty bleachers and started in on the first of their new, top-secret cheers.

> "Extra! Extra!
> Read all about it!
> Wolves're gonna win,
> No doubt about it!

"Late edition,
Just got in!
Headline says,
'Tarenton wins!' "

"Okay, okay," Ardith said, coming over with her clipboard in hand. "It sounds good. Mary Ellen and Angie, you did a nice job on the words. They're catchy. Now what we've got to do is come out of the line on this into a really sharp finale. What I want is all six of you doing triple cartwheels with the girls landing in splits — one girl facing in each direction. Walt, I want you to give Pres a stirrup hand-up so he can spring up onto your shoulders. The end I'm envisioning has Pres standing on Walt's shoulders, hands thrown up in the air, in the center of a starburst pattern made by the girls. Got it?"

The six of them rolled their eyes at each other. They dreaded seeing Ardith with her clipboard. She had a way of mapping out something outrageous on paper — the squad was supposed to form itself into a human Eiffel Tower or something like that — and then explaining it to them and acting like that meant it was as good as done.

"Well," Mary Ellen jumped in, "give us a while to run through it a few times and see if it works."

"Oh, it'll work beautifully," Ardith said, tapping her diagram with her finger. The thing was, Ardith was usually right. Sometimes her formations were nearly impossible to do, but once the squad finally pulled them off, they looked great.

This one took a lot of work, nearly two hours of run-throughs before they got it even close to right. When they finally did, they let it roll for Ardith, who sat midway up the bleachers, to give herself the vantage point of a representative Tarenton fan.

"Extra! Extra!"

they began. Angie had come up with the idea that, at the competition, they would each hold up a newspaper in their free hand, fakes printed up with TARENTON WINS! headlines.

"Read all about it!"

Underneath the bleachers, about six feet to the right of Ardith's sensibly shoed feet, there was a skulking presence. There, in the darkness, Vanessa Barlow was crouched with a notepad and a flashlight, scribbling away madly.

"Wolves're gonna win, no doubt about it," she whispered as she wrote the words. Then she stopped and thought, I wonder how much the Garrison squad would give to have these.

After practice, Nancy begged off with a headache, but the other three girls piled into Mary Ellen's mother's car.

"Hey," Walt said, coming out of the boys' locker room with Pres, and running into this mass exit. "Where are you all going?"

"To the mall," Mary Ellen shouted over her shoulder.

"Yeah," Angie said, "for a couple of rare, blissed-out hours of shopping and general goofing off. Which cheerleaders don't get to do much of these days."

"Can a guy come along?" Walt asked.

"No men allowed on this expedition," Olivia said. "We are cheerleading amazons from the planet Ultra — women desperate for clothes and makeup and gossip. We're going to land our spaceship at the Pineland Mall and go on a rampage. A man, especially a cute earthling like you, would only slow us down."

Walt hung his head in mock hurt.

"In that case, I guess I'll be forced into going home and watching college basketball on TV."

"I guess I'll have to join you," Pres said.

"Oh, poor babies," Mary Ellen said, knowing that watching basketball was precisely what the two guys wanted to do anyway.

On the way out to the mall, Mary Ellen, Olivia, and Angie felt cut loose from all the hard work of practices, all the tension surrounding games and, now, surrounding the competition. For the rest of the afternoon, they could let go of all that, and just be three ordinary girls.

They turned the radio up loud, especially when the latest Michael Jackson song came on. They sang along. They made incredibly stupid jokes and laughed hysterically at them. They pulled into Hamburger Heaven for Cokes and fries and a little time to just talk. Mary Ellen had something on her mind.

"What are we going to do about Nancy?" she said. She was beginning to really worry about her friend.

"Walt told me Pres is getting her involved in that handicapped athletics program his dad is setting up. Trying to take her mind off Ben," Olivia said.

"Well, bless the boy. Not a bad idea at all," Angie said. "The other thing she needs, though, is a new boyfriend."

"I could loan her Walt," Olivia said.

"Livvy! How can you say that?" Angie was astonished. "I thought you were the most solid couple in Tarenton."

"Oh, I guess we are," Olivia said. "I really do love him. But. . . ."

"But what?" Mary Ellen prompted. Clearly they were entering hard-to-talk-about territory.

"Oh, nothing," Olivia ducked.

"You can't 'oh, nothing' us, Livvy," Angie said. "We're your best friends."

Olivia sat in silence for a long moment, slowly eating a French fry. Finally, she said, "He's a terrible kisser."

The other two burst out laughing.

"Come on, you guys," Olivia pleaded. "I knew I shouldn't have told you."

"Okay, okay," Mary Ellen said, getting herself back in control. "I won't laugh anymore. It was just such a surprising thing to hear. Tell more. How terrible? Terrible how?"

"Oh, I don't know. He kind of smashes instead of smooshes. And he doesn't give me a chance to come up for air."

The other two thought about this for a minute.

"Kissing lessons clearly required," Mary Ellen said. Angie nodded in agreement.

"Oh, I can't," Olivia said. "He'd be so hurt."

"Not if you approach him gently," Mary Ellen said. "Patrick used to do this gnawing kind of thing on my lower lip. Like Woody Woodchuck. I straightened him out. Now he kisses so great I wish I hadn't taught him. It only makes it harder not to fall in love with him."

"Which you're not going to do, we know, we know," Olivia said, then fell into her own musings. "Kissing lessons, hmmm? Well, maybe."

By the time they got to the mall, it was late Saturday afternoon and the place was jammed.

"Well," Olivia said to the others, "now we know what every other kid in Tarenton does on Saturday."

"Where do you want to go?" Mary Ellen asked. Although she did some modeling for Marnie's, one of the stores in the mall, and had inherited some money from her Great Aunt Amanda, she was trying to put it away for her move to New York after graduation. She couldn't expect much financial help from her parents. If she was going to get out of Tarenton, she was going to have to do it herself. And that meant sacrifices *now*. She could not afford records or jewelry.

"I know," Angie said. "Let's go over to Neon and get some fluorescent socks."

"Good idea," said Olivia.

Mary Ellen could definitely not indulge herself in fluorescent socks.

She sighed and followed them through the mall. Maybe she would gain willpower on the way to Neon. Maybe. Well, probably not. By the time they got there, she had rationalized that two crummy pairs of fluorescent socks were not going to make the difference between getting to New York and not getting to New York.

Neon was the favorite store of most of the kids at Tarenton. The clothes and accessories they sold there were very hip and pretty cheap. Today, all three girls made a beeline for a rack of T-shirts with abstract art designs silk-screened on the front.

"Ooooh," Mary Ellen said suddenly, then sighed, looking over the top of the rack, toward the front of the store. "Chris Page."

Angie looked up and peered in the direction of Mary Ellen's gaze. There, near the front of the store, looking at a display of camouflage pants, was the most gorgeous hunk of guyhood she had ever seen. Tall, with high cheekbones, penetrating eyes, dark olive skin, and blond hair that nearly touched his shoulders.

"Who is he?" Angie asked. "This Chris what's-his-name?"

Both Mary Ellen and Olivia turned and looked at her incredulously.

"Angie!" Mary Ellen said. "Have you been on vacation in another solar system? Chris Page is only the most beautiful creature ever to grace the halls of Tarenton High."

"Well, I can see that. But where did he come from? The planet Krypton? He just slid down to Earth on a rainbow?"

"He transferred here a couple of weeks ago. I think you were home with a cold the day he got here," Olivia said. "Maybe that's why you missed the first flurry of excitement. Practically every girl in school went around a little goony that day."

"I did for sure," Mary Ellen said. "But since I'm not staying here one minute past graduation, there's no sense in my falling for anybody in Tarenton — not even someone who looks like he does."

"I suppose he's dated up from here to graduation," Angie said. "Or has Vanessa already snagged him for her trophy collection? I hear she and Donny Parrish are pffft. She's probably looking for a new conquest."

"I don't think it'll be him," Olivia said. "Mr. Page seems to be steering clear of entanglements with Tarenton girls. He's friendly enough to everyone, but always from a slight distance."

"Oh, well, it's hard to make friends when you're the new kid," Angie said, her attention back on the T-shirts. Who Chris Page was or wasn't interested in was only gossip to her. Guys who looked like blond Adonises were, she figured, out of her league.

When she was feeling up, Angie thought of herself as cute and high-energy. She knew she had nice eyes and great thick hair. When she was down, she worried that all anyone would notice about her was the zit on her chin, or the Poletti family thighs she was stuck with, which looked much better on her brothers.

Today she was feeling up — not up enough to think she could ever attract Chris Page's interest, and so she soon forgot about him — but definitely up enough to think she might look pretty cute in one of the modern-art T-shirts.

"Can anyone lend me two dollars?" she asked. "I'm a little short."

"You are a little short," Mary Ellen said, patting her on the head, "but we'll still let you hang out with us."

Olivia pulled a crumpled wad of bills out of the back pocket of her jeans and gave two to Angie. She counted out the rest to see if she had enough for the purse she wanted to buy — a little leather sack to wear tied around her waist. Mary Ellen held the line at two pairs of socks.

On their way to the cashier, Angie was counting out her money and adding it to the two dollars Olivia had given her and holding on to the T-shirt, not looking at all where she was going. All of which resulted in her bumping right smack into Christopher Page.

"Oh, hey, I'm sorry" he said, dropping to the floor to pick up everything Angie had dropped.

"Oh, no," Angie protested. "It was totally my fault. I'm walking around doing six things at once, when I really have trouble doing one thing at once. Really, you're in the clear on this one. Your insurance company can sue me."

"Why don't we call it no-fault," he said, smiling a smile that seemed to have about a hundred teeth in it. Then he held out his hand. Angie reached out and shook it. She felt electricity jump through her at his touch. At first she thought it was the power of his appeal, then realized it was static from the hi-tech carpeting. They both laughed at the same time.

"Well, I guess it's obvious I get a charge out of you," he said, smiling that smile again. Angie had to laugh. So this Adonis was a nice guy, too. Instantly she thought of him as a match for Nancy. Someone to take her mind off Ben.

"You're the new guy in town, I hear," she said. He nodded.

"How do you like it here?"

"Oh, it's nice, but I miss it back in California. I had a lot of friends. I like to surf. There isn't much of that here. It's kind of a rough change."

"It's tough on transfers," Angie said. "Everyone has their groups and friends set up. Hey, why don't you come over to the Presbyterian Church next Friday night? In the basement. They have these things called 'Friday.' They're kind of dances, but there's other stuff to do, too. A lot of the kids go over."

"Does that mean you're one of them?" he said. "If I came next Friday, would you be there?"

"Probably. Yeah, sure. And I'll bring my friend Nancy. I always come with her." This last part was a lie. Actually, Angie knew that Nancy usually didn't go to Fridays. But she would *next* Friday. Angie would make sure of that.

Outside the store, Olivia and Mary Ellen were lying in wait.

"What *happened?*" they both squealed at once. Angie took them by their arms and guided them along through the mall so she wouldn't have to stand there looking stupid when Chris Page came out of Neon.

"I talked him into coming to the next Friday," she told them when they were all the way to the earring booth.

"Oh, Angie," Olivia sighed. "He likes you."

"No, he just bumped into me. But he's going to fall for Nancy. Angie the Matchmaker is on the case."

CHAPTER 5

What am I doing here? Nancy asked herself as she stood on the wet tile floor at the side of the pool, wearing her old blue racing suit. In the water there were maybe a dozen swimmers, half of them doing laps in roped-off lanes; the rest working on their strokes, turns, and kicks.

Some of them were muddling through. Others, though, were really good.

I'm supposed to be a coach here? Some of these swimmers are way better than I am. I haven't even been competing seriously for a couple of years now. This is just dumb, she thought.

Then she took her gaze off the water and saw, all around the pool, temporarily abandoned wheelchairs, braces, crutches, and artificial limbs.

Although she had known before she came what this program was all about, the reality didn't sink in until this moment.

All these swimmers — even the really good ones — are handicapped, she realized.

This turned her perspective around. She wasn't here to be the best. She was here to help. If these people could put themselves on the line, so could she.

She was so deep in the middle of all this thinking that she didn't even hear the big wet footsteps coming up behind her. She felt a cold metal tap on her back, and turned abruptly to find a short, muscular guy, about twenty years old, with short black hair, holding a whistle that was attached to a lanyard around his neck.

What kind of nerd is this guy, tapping me with his whistle? she thought.

"You Nancy?"

"Yes."

"Eric Campbell. I'm in charge here. I just got a phone call saying you'd be coming. I really don't know anything about you or your swimming background."

"Well, I was on the junior varsity team at my old school. I haven't been team-swimming at Tarenton. I've been too busy on the cheerleading squad."

"What're your best strokes?" he asked, all business.

"I swam butterfly competitively, but I've got respectable times in freestyle."

33

He thought for a minute.

"I think I'll put you in with Greg Connors. He's working on his freestyle. He was an Olympic hopeful a couple of years back. Diving. Hit his head on the board on his way out of a tricky maneuver and hasn't been able to use his legs since."

"Poor guy," Nancy said.

"Yeah, well, don't say that to him. He won't hear it. He's the most positive person I've ever known. He's determined to be the fastest paraplegic in the water — going to try out for the next Special Athletics."

He started walking off. She assumed he wanted her to follow and so tromped off after him. When they got halfway down the pool he stopped and called out to one of the swimmers, a red-headed guy with freckles.

"Greg!" he shouted. "Santa's brought you a helper — Nancy, uh. . . ."

"Goldstein," she helped out.

"Greg's working on a power S-stroke, with alternate breathing. Oh, why don't you just get in and let him tell you," Eric said, walking off, shouting at someone lumbering through the water, "I want to see that head higher!"

Nancy shrugged at Greg, then took a shallow dive into the pool, coming up just in front of where he was treading water.

"Mr. Conversational," she said, meaning Eric.

"Oh, don't take it personally. He's just non-verbal. Talking is almost as difficult for Eric as walking is for me. Underneath his brusque exterior — "

"Beats a brusque heart," Nancy said, smiling.

"Something like that," Greg said, and laughed. "But underneath that lies an aorta of gold."

While they were kidding around, Nancy found she was noticing a lot about Greg. His hair was the darkest red imaginable, his eyes the brightest green. The combination was pretty sensational. She realized with a start that she had drifted off into reverie. Quickly, she pulled herself back to the reality of their being in about seven feet of water and the fact that she was supposed to be helping him.

"So, what can I do for you?" she said. "Eric said you're working on your freestyle."

"Mmm hmm," he said. "I'm trying to get a power stroke. My arms are all I've got in here. I'm doing an S-stroke with alternate breathing to add balance. Unlike most people's, my feet don't help much there."

She nodded thoughtfully, then said, "Why don't you do a few laps for me. I'll watch from water level, then underneath, then from the deck. I can't really give advice until I see what you've got going."

And so they began, with Nancy spotting him, offering tips, giving encouragement, demonstrating with her own stroke, and taking his hands and arms and putting them through the right moves.

It was hard work and took a lot of concentration. When Eric blew his whistle, calling, "Time's up," Nancy was exhausted.

"Good workout," Greg said. "And the first time I've had a personal coach. Usually Eric stops by when he can and gives me something to work on. But he's not nearly as attentive as you. Or as pretty."

Nancy dunked herself under water. When she came up, she explained, "Cools out my blushing."

Suddenly Eric was jumping into the water next to her.

"I'll help you get Greg out," he said. "Grab him under his right arm. I'll take the left."

She felt awful about this. In the water, she had nearly forgotten there was anything different about Greg. He was just a regular guy, kind of a cute one at that. Now, though, being hoisted out of the water, first onto the side of the pool, then into his wheelchair, he was transformed into someone else, someone who needed a wheeled contraption to get around. She realized that he must face this all the time — people thinking of him first as handicapped, then as a person.

"Too bad I can't stay in the water all the time," he said, as if reading her mind. "I'm best as a fish."

Nancy nodded, then said, "Too bad they don't have a better word for it. Handicapped is not a terrific label to have to wear." She was astonished at how easily she was able to talk with him about this. And yet somehow she knew she could be free with him; already there was a kind of understanding growing between them.

"There is. Some people call us 'differently abled,' which is definitely more positive than disabled or handicapped. Maybe too positive. I mean, something bad did happen to me. I am less abled than I was before the accident. Maybe you can think of a better word. Next time I see you, you tell me the word. We'll use it just between us." He smiled. "Now go hit the showers before you catch cold and are un-abled from coming back next week."

With that, he spun his chair around and wheeled off into the guys' locker room.

As she stood there watching Greg go, Nancy realized that, for the past two hours with him, she hadn't had one second's opportunity to think about Ben.

She waited for this to make her feel guilty, but it just didn't happen.

CHAPTER

On any Friday night in Tarenton, the basement of the Presbyterian Church was full of guys and girls — dancing, shooting pool, playing video games. Just hanging out, drinking Cokes, and talking. Making out in the darkened stairwell.

But on certain Friday nights, no one knew why — maybe it had to do with the tides or phases of the moon or interplanetary magnetism — absolutely *everyone* seemed to show up. The place was wall-to-wall dancing and gossiping, breaking up, and making up. An Event.

This was one of those Fridays.

"Boy," Angie said from the doorway, where she was on her way in with Nancy, "I wish I could get a videotape of all this, for instant replay later. There're more subplots going on here than

38

in three months' worth of *All My Kids*."

"Yeah," Nancy said in a tone of voice one step up from plant life. Since Ben's death, it had been impossible to get her excited about anything. Her friends understood this, but they expected her depression would gradually lift. Instead, this past week, she seemed to drift off even further. Her mind and feelings were clearly somewhere else.

Even in the face of this, Angie the Matchmaker had insisted that Nancy come along with her tonight. She was certain that one look at Chris Page would snap Nancy out of her funk. Angie craned her neck and scanned the pulsing crowd on the dance floor, trying to find him, but he wasn't there. She shifted her gaze to the place where Squid, Tarenton's number one — well, really, its only — rock group, was playing. He wasn't there, either. Then she looked toward the back of the room where there were tables and chairs, and kids were sitting and talking. Not there, either. Pres and Claudia were, though. Claudia seemed agitated.

"Honey," Pres said, knowing Claudia loved to be called honey, "you've got to know I'd much rather drive down to Florida with you than stay up here for a cheerleading competition."

"Then why don't you?" she said, her deep violet eyes welling up with tears, her lower lip pushing into a pout.

Pres took her hand.

"Because you can't make a six-person pyramid

with five cheerleaders. I just can't leave the rest of the squad in the lurch."

"But you *can* leave *me* in the lurch — is that it?" she said, slipping her hand out of his, wiping it on the leg of her black jeans, as if the sweat from his palm were a vaguely icky substance she didn't want on her own. Pres was beginning to see lately that there was a nasty edge to Claudia that appeared when she didn't get what she wanted.

"Claudia," he said, trying to be patient, "disappointing one person is bad, but not as bad as disappointing five."

"Sometimes one person is more important than the whole rest of the world. If it's the right person. Maybe I'm just not the right person."

"Oh, honey, of course you are," Pres said, desperately wishing he could get out of this conversation. In a flash, he saw his chance. Patrick Henley was just coming in through the back door. When he passed in front of Pres and Claudia, Pres stuck out his foot and curled a soccer hook around Patrick's ankle to stop him without Claudia seeing.

"Hey, Pres!" Patrick said, slapping a hand on Pres's shoulder. "And the fair Claudia." He bowed from the waist, his knight in shining armor routine.

"Looking for Mary Ellen?" Pres said.

"Actually, I was looking for you. I've got a little business proposition I'd like to discuss. As they'd say in *The Godfather*, I want to make you an offer you can't refuse. Not now, of course. Not in this delirious social setting, the highlight of life in Tarenton as we know it. But later."

"Well, you've got me curious," Pres admitted. "When do I get to hear this offer?"

Patrick shrugged. "I don't know. Why don't you throw on your grubbies and ride the garbage truck with me tomorrow morning? I bring a thermos of great coffee and I take the scenic route. We'll have plenty of time to talk, and you'll get to see what everybody's throwing out this week."

"Now *there's* an offer I can't refuse," Pres teased. "What time?"

"Oh, around five-thirty," Patrick said.

"*A.M.?*" Pres groaned in mock disbelief.

"Time, tide, and garbage wait for no man," Patrick said. "See you then, fella. I just spotted a girl I want to kiss before she knows what hit her." And with that he started making his way through the crowd to where Mary Ellen was shooting pool with Walt.

When he was out of earshot, Claudia turned to Pres and said, "I don't know what Patrick could possibly have in the way of a business proposition that would interest Preston Tilford III." Claudia was from a Virginia family as rich as Pres's own. She enjoyed being rich and looked forward to marrying Pres and continuing the lifestyle she'd become accustomed to. The thought of Pres having business contact with someone who drove a garbage truck made her slightly squeamish.

"I really don't think you ought to even bother talking to him tomorrow," she said.

Pres turned and looked at her and said, "If you'll pardon any possible rudeness on my part, Claudia, I'd just like to respectfully ask you to shut up."

Mary Ellen was demolishing Walt at the pool table. She only had to sink two more solids and the eight-ball to win. Olivia was sitting on a stool, leaning against the wall, intently watching the play. Although Walt was her boyfriend, she was secretly rooting for Mary Ellen. Girls didn't win enough. It was fun to watch it happen.

Olivia saw Patrick come up behind Mary Ellen. She put a finger up against her lips to warn him to be quiet. Patrick was the most impulsively romantic person in the world, at least whenever he was within a ten-foot radius of Mary Ellen. Olivia didn't want him spoiling her concentration, though. Romance could wait. This was a major game of pool.

It also turned out to be a short one. Mary Ellen sunk the last two balls, one straight into a corner pocket, one a three-bank shot into the side. Then, with a rake, she slid the eight-ball from the middle of the table neatly into a pocket at the end. Walt didn't even get a chance to pick up his cue again.

Taking *his* cue for action, Patrick bounded over to the winner, grabbed her in a hug, and spun her around into his arms and pulled her into a kiss that nearly gave off steam.

Which put Walt in a kissing frame of mind. He came up to where Olivia was sitting and pressed her back to the wall with one of his smashers.

She waited until he backed off and decided this was as good a time as any for Lesson One.

"Walt," she said gently.

"Hmmm?" he said, nuzzling her neck.

"It's about your kissing."

"What *about* my kissing?" he said, backing off abruptly.

"Well, it's wonderful, of course," she said. "Truly awesome, really."

"You think it's terrible," he said. "You think it's like kissing a horse. You've told all your girl friends. I'm the laughing stock of the whole class."

"Sweetheart, you're going way overboard on this. I'm just talking about a couple of tiny imperfections. And nobody knows — well, except Mary Ellen and Angie."

"Oh, no!" Walt moaned, throwing a hand melodramatically up to his forehead. "Angie Poletti and Mary Ellen Kirkwood think I'm a terrible kisser! Will I ever live this down? My reputation will be smeared for life. And not just here. Mary Ellen's moving to New York after graduation. Someday I'll be sitting on a subway in Manhattan and there among the other graffiti will be WALT MANNERS IS A ROTTEN KISSER. I can't bear it."

With that, he turned and walked off through

the crowd, which swallowed him up before Olivia could get off the stool and go after him. She knew that Walt, son of Tarenton's TV talk show hosts, had a flair for drama, but she was afraid that under this burst of histrionics just now was a really hurt person. Which had not been her intention. And now it was too late to undo the damage. She couldn't take back what she'd said. So, what was she going to do?

In the middle of a sweet conversation she was having with Patrick, Mary Ellen suddenly found herself being snatched by the hand and dragged by Olivia into the girls' rest room.

"What's up?" Mary Ellen asked when they were inside, standing by the row of sinks.

"It backfired," Olivia said, out of breath.

"What?"

"Telling Walt his kissing needs improvement."

"Oh, no," Mary Ellen moaned. "You didn't put it that directly, did you? Nobody's ego needs that."

"Well, what was I supposed to say?" Olivia asked, truly bewildered.

"Oh, I don't know. Something creative. You've been reading this really terrific new book — *Kissing Your Way to True Happiness and Aerobic Fitness*. Something like that. And in there are some hot new ways of kissing you'd never even think of, and would he like to try them with you."

Olivia just stood there in minor awe, watching Mary Ellen as she finished this rap and pulled a comb out of her jeans pocket and stood in front of the mirror, running it through her long blonde hair.

"Melon," Olivia said, "sometimes I think you're close to a genius."

This sentence got punctuated by the emergence of Vanessa Barlow from around the corner.

"Why *close* to a genius, Livvy?" she said. "I think Mary Ellen is at least a true genius, maybe a megagenius. And it's good advice she's giving you. I'm sorry to hear you're having trouble with Walt. Who'd have thought he'd be so . . . should we say *inept*?"

Mary Ellen ignored Vanessa, instead turning to Olivia and wincing.

"It's my fault," Olivia told her in a low voice. "I violated the Numero Uno rule of keeping secrets. Do not talk in the rest room. You never know who's lurking around where you can't see them."

"Oh, don't worry, Livvy," Vanessa said haughtily, fluffing her short black hair with her hands, then peering into the mirror as she freshened her lipstick. "I couldn't care less about your stupid boy troubles. I've got *important* things on my mind."

"I'm sure of that," Mary Ellen said, making sure her voice dripped with sarcasm.

"You don't consider college important?" Van-

45

essa sneered. "And I'm not talking Hillsborough J.C. I mean the Seven Sisters. Vassar, to be exact."

"Oh, yeah," Olivia said, "I heard one of their admissions counselors is supposed to be here next week interviewing."

"And *I* will be one of the interviewees," Vanessa said, now touching up her eyeliner. "Of course, the interview will be a mere formality. I could practically phone in and still be accepted."

"What makes you think that?" Olivia asked. "I thought schools like that were tough to get into."

"Not if you're a legacy," Vanessa said smugly.

"A what?" Olivia said.

"If your mother went there, or better yet, your mother and your grandmother, you're a legacy. They practically *have* to let you in."

"Not anymore they don't," Mary Ellen said in a sure voice, as though she really knew what she was talking about.

"What do you mean?" Vanessa said, turning her gaze slightly to look at Mary Ellen's reflection in the mirror.

"Everyone knows legacies don't count anymore. It's dog-eat-dog in college admissions nowadays. Now you have to fall back on the *one* surefire way to get in."

"Oh? What's that?" Vanessa said, trying to sound casual, but not quite succeeding. Mary Ellen knew she had her fish on the hook.

"Oh, come on, Vanessa. Really. Where've you been? I'm talking about The Slider."

"Oh, *that*," Vanessa said, then when she couldn't stand it any longer, "Okay, okay. I'll admit I don't know what The Slider is."

"Oh, sorry, Van," Mary Ellen said, "I wasn't being coy. I just assumed everyone knew about Sliders. It's really pretty simple. You go into the interview with your application in hand. The admissions counselor is behind a desk. She asks you to sit down, you chat a little, and then she asks to see your application. You slide it across the desk to her. She opens it up and finds a fifty-dollar bill clipped inside. And instantly your grade-point average isn't quite so important and she doesn't care that you haven't participated in one school activity in four years."

Vanessa listened to this with her mouth hanging open, then, when Mary Ellen was done, tried to close it and look unsurprised and knowing.

"Oh, yeah," she said, "I know that one. I just never heard it called The Slider before. I always hear of it as The Slipper. Well, I'd better get out of here. Much as I enjoy your company, there's someone out there I'm interested in conversing with a little." She stuffed her makeup and hairbrush in her miniscule shoulder purse and made a fast exit.

Olivia and Mary Ellen waited a couple of beats after the door was shut — just to make sure — before they burst out laughing.

"How did you ever concoct such an elaborate story right on the spot like that?" Olivia asked, then paused and added, "It *was* made up, wasn't it? The Slider?"

"One-hundred percent." Mary Ellen grinned.

"Do you think she'll fall for it?"

"Are you kidding?" Mary Ellen said. "I can already hear her piggy bank being smashed. I think I know Vanessa Barlow well enough to say that by Wednesday she'll have somehow come up with fifty dollars. Oh, my, can you see that Vassar woman's face when she sees that fifty?"

"Do you think it's too mean a trick?" Olivia asked.

"For Vanessa?" Mary Ellen said, raising an eyebrow. "It'll keep her occupied for a week. It'll distract her from stealing canes from the blind, or whatever rotten thing she'd be up to otherwise."

"You're right," Olivia said. "By the way, who do you think she's in such a rush to get to out there?"

"Christopher Page'd be my guess," Mary Ellen said. "I think he's the only guy in town she hasn't already hit on."

Vanessa never got a chance to make a move on Chris Page. He was barely through the door before Angie waved him over to where she and Nancy were taking turns on the Frogger video game.

"Hey," he said when he had cut through the crowd and gotten over to them. "I may be a snob about California, but I've got to say there's nothing quite like this out there."

"Oh," Angie said, "that's probably because kids out there have got so much stuff to do. I imagine they kind of spread out. In Tarenton on a Friday night, this is pretty much the only game in town. It's too dark to go over to the fence and watch the paint dry. And the Post Office is closed, so we can't go look at the new stamps. And — "

"I get you, I get you," Chris said, laughing.

While Angie was talking with Chris, Nancy just kept on playing Frogger, not looking up. Angie leaned toward her and gave her a swift elbow in the ribs.

"Hey, Nancy, I don't think you've met Chris Page yet."

Nancy turned around and smiled and said hi, but the kind of polite hi you give somebody's weird cousin from out of town, not the kind of hi you give the hottest new guy in Tarenton.

She wasn't rude exactly, just clearly not interested. And Chris didn't exactly seem struck by lightning himself. Still, Angie wasn't about to let the apparent lack of interest on both sides stand in the way of her grand scheme for these two. They just needed to get to know each other a little better. Luckily the next number Squid played was a slow one.

"Want to dance?" Chris said.

Angie sighed a sigh of relief until she realized he was asking her, not Nancy.

"Oh," she said, lifting her calf and rubbing it, "I'd love to, but I pulled a muscle in practice this afternoon. I'd better stay off it for tonight. We've got a game tomorrow. But Nancy's a dancing maniac, aren't you?" she said, turning to her friend, who by this time was back playing Frogger. She gave her another elbow in the ribs.

"Huh?"

"Dance? You? Him?" Angie said, pointing, caveman style.

"Uh, oh, okay," Nancy said and walked out onto the floor with Chris.

Angie watched with satisfaction as they danced under the waves of blue, then green, then red light. And with double satisfaction when they started talking with each other.

I wonder what they're talking about? Angie thought.

Out on the dance floor, Chris Page pulled back and looked down at Nancy.

"You don't really want to be out here, do you?" he said.

"It's not dancing. Or you. It's just that I lost somebody close to me recently, and I guess I'm not ready for anything else just yet."

He nodded.

"I heard about your boyfriend, and I'm sorry. And I think I understand where you're at. So please don't think I'm the one pushing you. It's

Angie who thinks you need a new boyfriend."

"I know. Well, I think it's *Angie* who needs the new boyfriend."

Chris Page grinned and said, "So do I. And I've got just the guy in mind."

CHAPTER

Patrick downshifted into second as he came around the turn onto the street where Pres lived, out on Fable Point. The ancient engine of the garbage truck chugged and sputtered against the silence of the wealthy neighborhood at dawn.

The brakes screeched as he pulled up into Pres's drive. Seeing Pres standing there, waiting for him, Patrick doubled over the wheel, laughing. Over his jeans and down jacket, Pres was wearing high rubber fisherman's wading boots held up with suspenders.

"We're only going to be picking up garbage," Patrick said, leaning out the truck window, "not slogging through it."

"Just wanted to be prepared for anything," Pres said, pulling open the door on the passenger

side and hoisting himself up into the truck. "My
first time in a truck."

"You're kidding," Patrick said, turning to look
at him in amazement.

"No," Pres said, slightly embarrassed, then,
making fun of himself a little, went on. "We
Tilfords generally travel lower to the ground.
You know, Mercedes. Porsches."

"Well, maybe you'll find you like it up here,"
Patrick said, rolling the truck out onto the road.
"It's a great view and a nice time of day and you
learn a lot about what's going on in Tarenton."

"How do you mean?" Pres said, not understanding.

"You find out a lot about people from their
garbage."

"Like?"

"Well, I can always tell when Mr. Anderson
the lawyer has been up all night working on a
tough case. His bags are full of coffee grounds.
And I know when the Caspers have had another
wild party. Sacks full of beer cans. I know Rachel
Robinson's got a crush on her piano teacher. Her
garbage is full of these half-torn pink notes.
'Darling Mr. Baker, When you play the Chopin
Etudes, it sends shivers down the spine of my
musical being.' "

"No," Pres said, unbelieving.

"It's true," Patrick said, crossing his heart with
a finger. "Garbageman's honor."

"This might be more interesting than I

thought," Pres said. "But, hey, where's the coffee — the big selling point of this adventure?"

Patrick reached down on the floor, pulled up a thermos, and handed it to Pres.

"Hope you like it with milk. It's already in there."

Pres barely had time to pour himself a cup and start to drink it when Patrick pulled up to the curb a few houses down from Pres.

"Oh, good," Pres said, "the Rudolfs. What do you know about them? I've always been curious. They keep to themselves so much."

"Well, he's writing some kind of novel about World War II," Patrick said, hopping out of the truck, pulling on heavy work gloves.

"No kidding," Pres said, following him around to the back of the truck. "Old Rudolf's a writer. Hmmm."

"Yeah. And he's doing it on a computer. His barrels are always full of those computer print-outs."

"Boy, you really *do* know everybody's business."

"Yeah, but I don't spread it around," Patrick said.

"You just told *me*."

"That's different. You're going to be my business partner."

"What are you talking about?"

"I'm expanding the operation," Patrick said, lifting one of the Rudolfs' barrels high on his shoulder and dumping its contents into the open back of the truck. "I've got a line on another truck, a big old bread truck. I can get it at a reasonable price. What I was thinking of was expanding into the moving business. There's quite a bit of money in it, I think." He stood facing the side of his truck and swept a hand across, imagining the new truck. "H&T's TLC Moving."

"TLC?" Pres said.

"Tender Loving Care."

"H&T's?"

"Henley and Tilford's."

"Ah. I see. But what makes you think I'd be interested?"

"Well, I wasn't sure. I needed a partner and you're one of my best friends. I also figured you might have a little money put away to help finance the truck. I also thought, well, I know your dad has your future all mapped out for you. I thought you might want to zip off the highway a little. Take your own side road."

When Patrick finished this speech he just stood looking at Pres, waiting for his response. For a long time there wasn't any. Then, finally, with a slow grin, Pres said, "Who'd get the moving and who, the garbage?"

Patrick threw his head back and laughed.

"Are you kidding? You think I'd give this up — and miss out on all the town secrets? Nope, you'd get the moving business. It'd be fun, Pres.

And lifting all those sofas would do great things for your biceps. You'd be even better in those pyramids."

"Argh. I'm getting a little worn down on pyramids. Ardith has really been working us like drones. We've got another extra practice this afternoon. And before that I've got to have lunch with my parents and Claudia. My mother's teaching her French cooking. My parents think Claudia's Wonder Girl. Sometimes it feels like they've already got us betrothed. Like in one of those countries where they pair you off when you're just kids and then when you're twenty you marry that person.

"I don't guess Claudia would much like me being a mover and hauler. What she's got in mind is me being a mover and shaker. You know. One of those guys they profile in *Fortune* magazine. 'Preston Tilford III has turned midsized Tarenton Fabricators into one of the top 500 companies. In his spare time, he plays polo and, with his charming wife, Claudia, hosts intimate dinners for fifty in their home, a small, renovated castle.' "

"They really do have you on a track, don't they?" Patrick asked.

"Yeah," Pres said, pulling off his knit cap and running his fingers through his dark blond hair. "But I think I might be about to jump the fence. Thanks for putting the burr under my saddle." He slapped Patrick's open palm and said, "Give me a little time to think about your offer."

* * *

"Uh, if it doesn't upset any of the chefs," Pres said, poking around at something on his plate that didn't look quite dead, "I wonder if someone could tell me what this is?" Genus and species will do, he thought.

"Raw oysters with macadamia nut and blue cheese sauce," his mother announced proudly. "Claudia made it out of the *Très Nouvelle Cuisine* cookbook."

Pres gulped and pushed the plate slightly away from himself. He looked across the table at a radiant Claudia, beaming with accomplishment.

"Looks great," Pres said, "really great. And so original. But, gosh, I guess I forgot to mention to anyone that Ardith has forbidden us to eat any seafood while we're in training for the competition. She says it affects the inner ear and she doesn't want anyone turning up with balance problems." He was lying wildly. He didn't really think anyone could possibly believe a word of this. He was just saying anything to get out of eating one of these oysters.

It was his dad who got him off the hook.

"Well," he said now, "I don't want to incur the wrath of Ardith Engborg. If she's got you kids on a program, I don't want to be the one to go against it. I can deal with angry board chairmen and furious corporation presidents, but the wrath of Ardith Engborg is more than I can stand up to. We'll just have to enjoy these ourselves and let Pres start in on the main course."

"Lamb patties in raspberry sauce," Claudia

said sweetly as Pres felt himself going green around the gills.

After lunch, Pres and Claudia went into the old ballroom, where Pres kept his stereo equipment.

"I've got a new record I want to play for you," he told her, pushing the door closed behind them and pulling her into a lingering kiss at the same time. Claudia was a very hot kisser. Even when he wasn't at all sure she was the girl he wanted to spend the rest of his life with, he was very sure she was the girl he wanted to be kissing. Plus, when he came out of a kiss with Claudia, there were those big violet eyes looking at him and that soft southern voice saying, "Honey."

"Honey," she said now.

"Hmmm?" Pres said, wanting to get back to kissing.

"What did Patrick want to talk to you about this morning?"

Inside, Pres groaned. Those violet eyes didn't miss a trick, and behind that cooing southern exterior was a mind like a steel trap. There was no sense trying to beat around the bush with her.

"He's buying another truck, expanding into the moving business. He thought I might be interested in being partners with him."

Claudia threw back her head and laughed in that lighthearted way he usually loved. At the moment, though, it was incredibly irritating. He walked away from her and put his new Don Henley album on the stereo.

"Thought you might like this," he said. "I picked it up at Mercer Records the other day." He lowered the stylus onto the revolving record and turned the volume on the amp up to nine. To close the conversation.

Claudia came over and turned it back down to three, bit Pres on the ear, and asked, still in her honey-dipped voice, "So, of course you told him to go fly a kite. I do hope you did it tactfully, so you didn't hurt his feelings too bad."

He broke free of her hand on his arm and said, "I told him I'd think about it."

"But you can't be serious. A Tilford hauling somebody's old sofas and junk around? Think how it would look. And besides, where would you find the time? Pretty soon you'll be graduating. And then you'll want to spend the summer getting familiar with things at your dad's place. Then in the fall, Princeton, I'm sure."

"Maybe."

"Why, sugar, what can you possibly mean?" she said. "I won't have any of those negative thoughts around here. Of course you'll get in."

"I meant maybe I won't *accept* if I do get in," he said.

"Why, Pres Tilford, whatever can you mean?" she said, the honey in her voice turning slightly acid.

"I mean that everybody's got such a clear plan

for me, but nobody asks me what *I* want."

"Why, sweetie, all we want is the very best for you."

"Yeah," Pres said sarcastically, "*your* idea of best."

"Pres," she said, putting her hands on his shoulders and looking him deep in the eyes, "I've always thought we thought alike, that we agreed on what's best. We're both used to being rich. This is the life we know, the life our families have prepared us for. We're happy being rich. What are you going to do — drive this moving truck and rent a crummy apartment and come home at night and watch black-and-white TV while sitting in your thrift-shop chair?"

"I just might, Claudia," he said, wanting to wipe that smirk off her face. "I just might."

"Pres is having a little tantrum," she said. "Your mother warned me about them. Maybe I should just skedaddle out of here and let you stew for a while. Then, when you're feeling back to your old, reasonable self, why don't you give Claudia a little jingle?" She kissed him on his burning cheek and then whisked herself away.

Pres stood stock still in front of the stereo until he heard the door shut behind her.

Don't hold your breath waiting for that call, he thought.

CHAPTER

"E-NUN-CI-ATE!" Ardith shouted at the Tarenton cheerleading squad from her perch up in the bleachers. "You sound like you've all got mouths full of oatmeal, which I'm sure you don't. And if you do, get rid of it. Oatmeal's got too many carbohydrates for this stage in your training."

At this, all six of them cracked up. Ardith even smiled at herself. Something they all liked about her was that she usually knew when she'd really gone over the line.

"All right, all right," she shouted now. "Let's try it again without the oatmeal!"

They stood facing her, looking like dancers in their shorts and leg warmers and sweat shirts. With mimeographed sheets in hand, they shouted back at her, separating the words as much as they could while at the same time screaming them.

> *"Jump, jump, jump,*
> *Sink, slam, dunk!*
> *Come on, Wolves,*
> *Dunk it in!*
> *Two more points,*
> *And Tarenton wins!"*

"Better, better," Ardith said, nodding. "Now, for the formation I've got in mind to go with this one. On 'Jump, jump, jump,' I want three different jumps, with two of you doing each of them. That is, on the first 'Jump,' I want Mary Ellen and Olivia doing split jumps. On the second one, I want Walt and Angie doing pike jumps. On the third, Pres and Nancy doing straddle-toe jumps. On 'Sink, slam, dunk,' I want the same sort of thing, only with a stag jump, a banana, and a full-C. And then. . . ."

But the squad was already groaning too loudly for her to go on.

"Come on, kids. I know it sounds a little complicated, a bit of a stretch, but you'll see. When we put this baby together, we're going to have one incredible cheer. And incredible cheers are what we're going to have to have at the tri-state competition. Do you think that right now in Deep River and Northfield and Kensington they're working out namby pamby little cheers? Do you think they're sitting in their folding chairs sort of waving their pompons around a little? Give me a break!"

"All *right*!" Walt said, jumping up in a stag jump. "Let's forget those child labor laws and give Ardith a break!"

And the rest of them got behind him and into working on the cheer. Which took almost four hours to get even roughly down.

Of course, it only took Vanessa Barlow a fraction of that time, once again kneeling underneath the bleachers, to get the cheer and formation down in her little black notebook.

" 'Jump, jump, jump,' " she said to herself. "They're going to jump at that competition when they see the Garrison squad doing this cheer before they do. Too bad they run the competitions alphabetically. Too bad 'G' comes before 'T,' Garrison before Tarenton. I guess they're just going to have to concede defeat and take their pompons and go home. Poor kids. And to think I wanted to be one of them once. Well, I wouldn't want to be a Tarenton cheerleader at that competition. I just hate being embarrassed."

It was past five when Angie finally finished showering and blowing her hair dry and changing back into a beat-up pair of cords and an old peach-colored crew neck her older brother had outgrown. The locker room was empty by now.

She was always the last one ready, and today had just told the others to go on without her. Mary Ellen was going out with Patrick tonight; Livvy, with Walt. Nancy hadn't even stopped off to shower. These days she usually ducked home right after practice.

Angie checked herself in the mirror on the way out.

Pretty scruffy, Poletti, she thought. But then all you've got on tap tonight is making a pizza and catching a movie on cable with the folks. A date you don't exactly have to dress up for.

She pushed open the door and found herself in the darkened main corridor of school. They only kept a few lights on over weekends.

And so she was startled by the sudden presence of someone saying, "Hi."

She turned around. It was Chris Page.

"Oh," she said, putting her hand on her heart, an old Italian gesture she'd picked up from her Grandma Poletti. "You gave me a start."

"No major coronary damage, though?" he said.

"I don't think so," she responded, and laughed. She was always laughing around him, even when he wasn't really being all that funny. "Do you always skulk the halls on weekends?"

"I'm just playing lost and found. Someone left this scarf in my car after I dropped you and Nancy off last night. I was thinking it might be yours."

Angie took the blue and green tartan wool from him and said, "Nope, this is Nancy's." She started to hand it back. "I guess you'll want to give it back to her in person. I can give you her address in case you don't remember from last night."

"Oh, well, maybe you could just give it to her."

Isn't that sweet? Angie thought. He's so shy about seeing her.

"Okay, sure," she said. "I can do that. I'll run by there on my way home. She's probably there. She stays home a lot these days, brooding about Ben. If you want my opinion, what she needs is someone new to take her mind off the past."

He thought about this and nodded. "You're probably right."

He means himself, she thought. But he's worried it's too soon, that Nancy isn't ready to start seeing someone else.

"I think the longer she broods like this," Angie said, "the further she's going to spin out in this depression of hers. Whoever rode her way would be a knight in shining armor."

"Well," Chris said, trying to change the subject, "there aren't many knights around these days. Like they say, chivalry is dead. But I'd still like to offer you a ride home. And you'd better take me up on the offer. It's pouring outside."

"Really?" Angie said. "What a weird spring this is. Just when you think it's getting nice and warm for a day, it starts to snow, then rain, then snow again. The old snow sandwich."

"Wow," he said, scratching his head, "it's funny, you saying that. I used just that image in this poem I was writing the other day. Coming from California, I can get pretty inspired by this weather. It's so much more dramatic than what I'm used to."

"You write poetry?" she said, amazed. She thought guys who looked like he did just kind of hung out, being gorgeous. She hadn't thought that they might also have an inner life.

"Guilty as charged," he said.

"Me, too," she said, almost whispering it. She'd never told anyone about her poems, not even Mary Ellen. Why was she telling him? Well, he was *so* easy to talk to. She was never nervous around him. Probably because there was no possibility of them getting involved. It made him more of a friend, and friends were always so much easier to talk to than guys you were after. "I think my poems are probably pretty terrible," she added. "Well, most of them, anyway. I mostly write them as kind of a way to figure out my feelings. They're kind of little letters to myself."

"Hey," he said, smiling. "I call mine 'journal entries.' We seem to be on the same wavelength a lot. Do you notice that?"

"You mean like kindred spirits?" she said.

"Something like that. I was afraid I wouldn't find anybody like that here."

He needs a friend, Angie thought. Even incredibly gorgeous guys need someone to just talk to once in a while. They can't just always be looking great and driving girls crazy. They have to stop sometimes and communicate with somebody. They need a buddy. That's what he wants me to be. His buddy.

"Hey," he said softly now, "you want that ride or not?"

She smiled up at him. "Let's go."

On their way out, he turned to her, putting a hand softly on her shoulder.

"Say, Angie," he said. "Would you ever let me read your poems? In exchange for mine? Just the ones we think are best? Would you trust me that much?"

By now they were almost to the front entrance of the school. The lights from outside streamed in, illuminating his astonishingly blue eyes as he looked down into hers. For just a second, this took Angie's breath away. For just a moment she forgot all about being buddies. But she caught herself quickly. Forget it, Angie, she told herself.

"Okay," she told him. "I'll do it. It'll be very scary, but real interesting to let another person see them."

By then, they were out the door. The parking lot was empty except for Chris's Camaro and one other car — a little green Spitfire that was just pulling out, sputtering its way out of the lot. There was only one old sports car like that around Tarenton High. Vanessa Barlow's.

"Hmmm, that's weird," Angie thought out loud.

"What?" Chris said.

"I don't know. First you, now Vanessa. Maybe it's a new trend. Maybe everyone's started hanging around school on weekends."

CHAPTER

"Come on. More. I want to see those arms really stretch as you cut into the water," Nancy said, shouting over the din in the pool, taking Greg's hands and tugging hard on them. "There. Do you feel that when you do it yourself?"

"Not that much," he admitted.

"You should. And remember to angle your hand, thumb down, as it slices into the water. Like this."

She took Greg's hand and showed him. She kept finding it was so much easier to show this kind of thing rather than try to explain it. The problem was, it kept putting her into a lot of physical contact with the person she was coaching. In this particular instance, it left her holding that person's hand.

Both she and Greg got embarrassed about this at the same moment. They looked down at their entwined hands, then sheepishly up at each other.

"Say," Greg said, "weren't you going to come up with a better word for me. You know, instead of handicapped?"

"Mmm hmm," Nancy said. "And I did. Hydra-abled."

"*Hydra-abled?!*" Greg said. "What's that?"

"A little Latin, a little English. In means you move well in the water."

He smiled shyly and said, "I like it."

Which threw them both back into another silence, from which they were saved by the bell. Or, rather, by Eric's piercing whistle ringing through the air, signaling the end of this week's session.

"I think I'm going to steal that whistle when he's not looking sometime," Greg said.

"Great idea," Nancy said. "We can replace it with a little set of chimes. Then he'll have to go bong-bong-bong real nice and soft. Zen coaching."

Greg laughed.

Nancy loved it when he laughed. It made his green eyes light up. She didn't have much time to dwell on this, though. In one instant, Eric was in the pool with them, helping her get Greg out. In the next, Greg was wheeling toward the showers talking to Eric about tryouts for the regional Special Athletics meet coming up. He waved good-bye over his shoulder to Nancy as he opened the steel door to the guys' locker room and wheeled in.

She stood there, hopping on one foot and shaking her head, trying to get the water out of her right ear, and finding herself surprisingly hurt that Greg hadn't stayed on to talk longer, or at least to a say a real good-bye.

Get a grip, she told herself. This is just some guy you've been assigned to help. It doesn't matter if he likes you or not. This is about swimming. Nothing else.

She was about to leave, then thought, What's the hurry? Pres hadn't been able to come today and so she didn't have to rush to get a ride with him. She looked over her shoulder back at the pool, which was empty now, settling into a glasslike plane. It was too tempting to resist. She looped her towel back over the bar and dove in.

After her swim, she headed for the showers and took a long hot one and washed and blew her hair dry. All of this took quite a while, and so she was astonished, coming out of the locker room, to find Greg sitting there in his wheelchair waiting for her.

"What . . . ?" she started.

"I got so intense talking with Eric about the tryouts, I didn't get to say a proper good-bye to you."

"Oh, that's okay," she said.

"No, it's not. And I think the least I can do to make amends is take you to heaven. Hamburger Heaven, that is."

"B-b-but how?" Nancy stammered. She realized in a flash that she only knew Greg in the water. That's why she thought of him as hydraabled. In the water, everything was simple. But going for a hamburger? How would they get there? She had come by bus. Could she get him on one? And then what would they do once they got to Hamburger Heaven? She tried to remember if the space between the tables there was wide enough for him to wheel through.

Her panic must've shown through her eyes. He picked it up right away.

"Hey, don't worry," he said. "It's cool. I've got the situation covered. Come on, I've got my car outside."

"Your *car*?" she said, incredulous.

"Sure. You think these are my only wheels? Come on, I'll show you."

She was amazed at the sequence of small events that happened from there. With crisp efficiency, Greg first wheeled around and opened the door on her side of the car, then went around and opened his. In a rapid shift, he hoisted himself out of his wheelchair and into the driver's seat. Then he reached out and collapsed the chair and hauled it into the well behind his seat back. He shut the door smartly and put the key in the ignition.

Nancy gave him an alarmed look.

"Don't worry," he said. "Here. See. Handbrake and gas lever on the column. You think you footed folks are the only ones who can drive?"

He grinned at her and took her hand across the seat. "Trust me, Nancy. I'll never get you in an awkward spot."

"Oh, I didn't think you would. I was just boggled there for a minute trying to figure out all the logistics of getting a hamburger with you."

"It is pretty boggling at first," he said. "But I've been getting through all these new situations for more than a year now. I think I've got the basic ones knocked. To save time and energy, though, I may let you go in and get our burgers."

"You've got a deal," Nancy said, squeezing his hand before he took it back to shift into reverse to get them out of the parking space.

It being early Sunday afternoon, Hamburger Heaven wasn't too crowded yet. Greg slid the car into a space close to the door. As soon as he'd parked, Nancy jumped out and came around to his side. She tapped on the window and made a circle with her finger indicating he should roll his window down.

"Carhop service," she said, pretending to be holding a pad and chewing gum. "What'll it be?"

"Uh, how about two double cheeseburgers, a large fries, and a strawberry shake?"

"Ah, the Diet Delight. Of course."

He started to pull out his wallet, but Nancy put up her hand.

"Nope. Coach's treat. You can buy the celebration dinner after you bring home a medal from the regionals."

She walked into Hamburger Heaven, which was almost an archaeological artifact, a perfectly preserved piece of the fifties. The same jukebox near the front door, that had been there when the parents of today's Tarenton kids — and some of *their* older brothers and sisters — were teenagers. The booths were still upholstered in that blue vinyl with little sparkles in it. The hamburgers were still patted into shape by hand — many by the hand of Mr. Peterson, who had run the place for the past thirty-plus years. Nancy loved Hamburger Heaven. She thought it said yet another thing about how attuned she and Greg were that he'd suggested they come here.

As she was thinking these thoughts, making her way through to the order counter, she almost didn't notice Vanessa Barlow sitting alone in one of the booths, looking over a sheaf of printed forms and slowly sipping a Coke. She saw Nancy coming and said hi as she passed. Nancy stopped, curious about the forms.

"Hi. Watcha doin'?" Nancy asked.

"Oh, just working on my application to Vassar. Their admissions counselor is coming to Tarenton tomorrow."

"Oh, well I'm sure you'll get in."

"Really?" Vanessa was usually so awful to everyone that they were awful back. So she wasn't used to compliments like this. And she was only getting this one because Nancy was one of the nicest girls in Tarenton. She almost couldn't be un-nice. Even though she didn't like Vanessa, when she'd seen her pondering those forms, she could tell Vanessa was worried or nervous. Nancy's natural instincts were to try to make people feel better. Even Vanessa.

"Yes, really," Nancy said now. "I think you've got a lot of poise. The Vassar person will be impressed. So don't worry."

"Well, I'm not, of course," Vanessa said haughtily. "I've got the grades and the activities, and my mother went there, which still must count for something. And of course, I've got Mary Ellen and Olivia's little trick."

Nancy didn't know what she was talking about. She mostly just wanted out of this little conversation. She had some hamburgers to get. And so she just said, "Oh yeah, definitely follow their advice. I do all the time. They never steer me wrong. See you later, Vanessa. And good luck."

She's so nice, Vanessa thought, watching Nancy walk away. I hate the idea of her being hurt by my little bit of sabotage. And Mary Ellen and Olivia — helping me get into college that way. They didn't have to tell me about The Slider. I've probably been wrongheaded, stealing their cheers. Thinking about giving them to the squad at Garrison. I'm going to stop. And I'll tear up the ones I already know. Tomorrow, when I've got time after my interview.

Nancy came back to Greg's car carrying two paper bags. She got in the car and began opening them up.

"Doesn't swimming make you so hungry you can't believe it?" she said.

He nodded, already pulling fries out of the bag and munching on them.

"Ravenous," he said. "If I were a distance swimmer — you know, the English Channel and stuff like that — they'd have to keep a food tray around my neck all the time."

"You know, I really think you're turning into a great swimmer. You have a pretty good chance at the regionals. Your times aren't that far off now, and we've still got a few weeks to go."

He took a long pull on the straw stuck in his shake and just looked at her. Finally he said, "Do you think of me just as a swimmer, just as the guy you coach?"

Nancy shook her head and said, "No. It's more than that now."

"One more question, then," he said. "Do you think of me as a cripple?"

She looked up sharply in the middle of biting into her fish sandwich. She was about to say, Oh no, but could see from his eyes that he wanted truth, not flattery, that something was on the line behind the question. And so she tried to give him what he was looking for.

"You can't use your legs. That makes you different from most people. It makes your life a more complicated business. It makes you an odd man out. When we're in the pool together, I forget it almost totally. Out here in the real world it comes up too often to forget it, but I guess I never think of you as a cripple. I guess I think of you as brave, braver than I am. I think I'd have caved in if it had happened to me. I guess — I don't know how to say this without getting embarrassed — I guess you're the first really heroic person I've ever known."

During this last part of what she had to say, he had stopped eating fries, stopped sipping on his shake, and just looked at her. When she was finished and fell silent, he leaned across the pile of waxed papers and cups and fries and half-finished burgers and put his hand around the back of her head. He pulled her toward him and kissed her long and seriously. Seriously enough for Nancy to realize that she'd never been *really* kissed before, not like this. Long enough for several people — including Vanessa, then Walt and Olivia — to pass by the car and get a good view of the action. Nancy didn't see any of them. When she pulled back and opened her eyes and caught her breath, all she saw was Greg Connors. And, "Oh, boy," was all she could find to say.

Three cars down from Nancy and Greg, Walt and Olivia, over onion rings and Cokes, were discussing this new romance mere minutes after it had begun.

"Who is he?" Olivia wondered.

"Dunno," Walt said. "I don't recognize him. He looks older than high school. I don't suppose we can just go over and ask."

"Walt!"

"Okay, okay. I guess it comes from being the child of TV interviewers. Your first instinct when you're curious about someone is to push a microphone in his face and start asking questions. Wow, though, that really was some kiss."

"I'll say," Olivia agreed.

"Uh, well," Walt said, looking first out the window, then down at the steering wheel, "is that what you had in mind for us?"

Olivia nodded.

"More or less."

"I think I'm beginning to get your point," he said, smiling, then smothered the grin to get mock serious and say, "But this isn't going to be easy. It's going to take a lot of work to kiss that good. We're going to have to practice, practice, practice, as Ardith would say. And double practice on Saturday nights."

"So," Olivia said, reaching over and pulling off Walt's cap, then grabbing onto the lapels of his jacket, bringing his face close to hers, "let's get started."

And when Greg Connors pulled his car out of the Hamburger Heaven lot, it was Nancy's turn to be the astonished observer.

"My, my," she said. "Look at Walt and Livvy. I guess the old flame is still burning pretty high."

CHAPTER

10

All of the cheerleaders had lunch at noon, except for Pres and Mary Ellen, who had been done in by the scheduling computer and drawn late lunch at quarter to one.

"Well, at least waiting this long to eat lowers your standards," Pres was saying to Mary Ellen on Monday as they inched along through the cafeteria line.

"Speak for yourself," she said, taking only a carton of skim milk. She'd brought her own lunch from home: carrot and celery sticks and cottage cheese. She'd gained a few pounds lately, which would simply not do for an aspiring model.

"I enjoy eating the cafeteria food, in a weird sort of way," he said. "I see it as a small, personal test of courage. Like this," he went on, taking a plate of something murky. "Is this hamburger in here, or tuna? Are these red things tomatoes or pimentos? This is for sure macaroni, but that's the only thing you *can* say for sure about this particular large glop. The smaller green glop next to it is an even deeper mystery. A mystery of the ages. Animal, vegetable, or mineral? Vegetable would be my guess, but lima beans or just peas that have been squashed beyond recognition? And with it, a slice of this nice white bread."

"Uh," Mary Ellen said, leaning over the counter for closer inspection, "I think that's pound cake."

"Whatever it is, I, Pres Danger-is-my-middle-name Tilford, will eat it."

They paid the cashier and started looking around for somewhere to sit.

"Ah," Pres said, "the gracious atmosphere of Le Café Tarenton. A bustling little bistro of familiar faces."

"Which of those friendly faces do you want to sit with today?" she asked.

"None, really," he said, getting serious. "If you can stand it, I'd like to tell you my troubles. Is there a space anywhere where we can be alone?"

She scanned the room.

"Over there, by the windows. See?"

They wound their way over and sat down with their trays.

"So?" Mary Ellen said, opening her carton of milk. "What can I do for you? As Lucy in 'Peanuts' says, 'The psychiatrist is in.' "

"I don't know if I need a shrink so much as a career counselor, and maybe a marriage counselor."

"Let me guess," Mary Ellen said, opening her plastic container of cottage cheese, "you've decided you want to become a forest ranger, but Claudia's allergic to wood."

"Is that cottage cheese? How can you eat that stuff?" he said. Then when she wouldn't dignify this with an answer, he went on. "Well, it is sort of like that. Patrick wants me to go into business with him."

"The moving thing?"

"He told you?"

She nodded, biting into a carrot stick.

"Well, I'm not sure, but I'd kind of like to give it a try. I know my parents will pull a total freak-out. I mean, going into the moving business is not exactly part of their career plan for the next president of Tarenton Fabricators. But I'd hoped Claudia would get behind the idea."

"She didn't, I gather," Mary Ellen said, now onto a celery stick.

"She laughed in my face. Have you ever had anyone laugh in your face? It's not a pleasant experience. You know, I'm beginning to see a new side of Claudia. When things don't go exactly the way she wants, she's got a nasty edge to her."

"Maybe it was just her initial reaction. Sometimes people back down from first positions."

Pres thought about this as he chewed on a mouthful of Turkish Jambalaya, which was how

81

the mysterious main dish was billed on the cafeteria wall menu.

"Maybe," he said. "But I'm getting this bigger picture — and this is just one instance — that what she likes isn't so much me, but who I am and how much money I have and where I'm headed."

"Do you really think that?" Mary Ellen asked.

"Well, what do you think? If I were suddenly poor and worked on the assembly line at the plant and wasn't going to Princeton, do you think Claudia would still be my girl?"

"Probably not," Mary Ellen admitted. And was set to thinking, asking herself the reverse question: If Patrick were rich and destined to become a captain of industry and headed for an Ivy League school, would she still be determined not to fall in love with him?

Was this fair? Didn't it make her as crummy as Claudia? If she loved Patrick, why should all the Patrick-surroundings matter one bit? And she did love him. Who was she kidding? And wasn't love the important thing? If you found someone you really cared about, shouldn't that come before some half-baked fantasy about a modeling career in New York? And if she really loved Patrick, even if there were problems around it, shouldn't she at least tell him she loved him?

Yes, she decided and, overwhelmed by the emotion of the moment, began to cry right there at the lunch table.

"Oh, Mary Ellen," said Pres, who hadn't been

party to any one of the thoughts flipping through her head, and thought she was crying over his problem. "I knew you'd be sympathetic, but not *this* sympathetic. Please don't cry about it. I'll work it out. I'll have another talk with her."

Embarrassed and not wanting to explain the whole thing, Mary Ellen just kept pulling paper napkins out of the metal dispenser on the table and wiping her eyes and blowing her nose until she was dry again.

"Pres," she said when she'd pulled herself together, "can I ask you a favor?"

"Anything, Melon. Anything."

"Can I have that piece of pound cake? I'm starving."

CHAPTER 11

At precisely two-seventeen on Monday afternoon, Vanessa Barlow emerged from Room 317, where she had been meeting with the admissions counselor from Vassar.

She emerged at a speed that broke the world's record for fastest run from Room 317 to the locker shared by Mary Ellen Kirkwood and Olivia Evans in the two-hundred wing of the school.

Since Mary Ellen and Olivia had gotten out of their last classes at two-fifteen, the timing was unfortunately perfect for them to witness the approach, at unbelievable speed, of Vanessa, whose face was approximately the color of a ripe beet. When she got about two feet from Mary Ellen and Olivia, she stood for a moment, shaking, before she could even begin to speak.

"What is it, Vanessa?" Mary Ellen said. Although she had forgotten about the phony advice she'd given Vanessa, it was coming back to her pretty fast now.

"Hi, Vanessa," Olivia said, also pretty sure of what was coming.

"How *could* you?!" Vanessa finally sputtered. "How could you two rotten, evil Cheerleaders from the Black Lagoon tell me such an awful lie?"

"Uh, I'm not sure what you mean, exactly," Mary Ellen said, buying time.

"You know full well what I mean," Vanessa said. "How could you ruin my chances for getting into Vassar by luring me into that slimy lie?"

"You mean it didn't work?" Olivia said, acting incredulous. "She didn't take the fifty? Those admissions counselors must be getting more honest these days."

"Didn't take it?" Vanessa said. "Is that all you think happened? The woman threw me out of the office. She took the fifty and tore it in little tiny pieces and let them flutter all over the floor in front of me, then she threw me out. It was the single most humiliating moment of my entire life. If I live to be a hundred, I won't forget it. Nor will I forget who put me up to it. Nor will I ever forgive you."

Both Mary Ellen and Olivia just stood there at first, silent and guilty. Finally Mary Ellen spoke.

"Vanessa, I'm sorry. Really. It was a practical joke. I guess I just didn't think there would be such terrible consequences. Didn't you tell her someone had put you up to it?"

"What would it matter? I believed you. You were just fooling around, but I really was trying to buy my way into college."

"Hey," Olivia said, "I'm sorry, too."

"Sorry? What good is sorry now?" Vanessa wailed. "I missed the chance of a lifetime."

"Calm down, Vanessa," Mary Ellen said, feeling really bad now. "We'll make it up to you. We'll do all your applications for you until you get in someplace else you like. I'll even go to the interviews for you, if you want. All you'll have to do is sit home and watch TV and we'll get you into college."

Vanessa didn't bother responding to this. Instead she glared at them with eyes full of fire, and said, "Watch out, cheerleaders. I'll get my revenge."

And with that, she turned on her heel and stomped off down the hall.

When she'd gone, Mary Ellen and Olivia stood in silence, looking at each other. There was no use being sarcastic about this. They were in the wrong and Vanessa had a right to be furious. And a furious Vanessa was a dangerous item.

"I feel awful," Olivia said.

"Me, too," Mary Ellen admitted. "I thought it was funny when we did it. You know, getting back at Vanessa for how awful she's been a million times. But I guess revenge isn't really sweet. Unless you've got weird taste like hers."

"And now we're in trouble, aren't we?" Olivia asked.

"Deep," Mary Ellen said. "We'll have to tell the others. She's going to be up to her worst now, and Vanessa's worst is not something I enjoy dealing with. But it's not Vanessa I'm worried about at the moment," she went on, slamming her books into the locker and pulling out her jacket. "She's not the only one I've been unfair to. And the other person is much more deserving of niceness. So I've decided to give him a little."

"Patrick?" Olivia said.

"Mmm hmm. I'm going to try to find him and see if he'll let me walk him home from school. It rained today so maybe I'll be able to find a puddle to throw my coat over so he can walk across. If I had some rose petals with me, I'd strew them in front of him as he walked."

"Wow," Olivia gasped. "What brought all this on?"

"I'm not sure. I'm either coming to my senses, or going completely crazy."

While this was happening at the lockers in the two-hundred wing, in the one-hundred wing, Angie was standing by Walt's locker, her mouth hanging open at the news he was telling her.

"Well, who *was* this guy?" she said in disbelief.

Walt pulled on his big Arctic explorer fur hat, another piece of his eccentric wardrobe.

"I don't know. I thought you might. Red hair, freckles. Looked like Joe College. Definitely not high school."

"Maybe he was just someone from that handicapped program. Someone who'd given her a ride back to Tarenton. Maybe he got something in his eye and she was helping him get it out."

"Angie," Walt said, slamming his locker door shut and giving it a swift soccer kick when it stuck, "I may not be Mr. Perceptive, but I can tell the difference between someone getting something out of someone's eye and two people in a major kiss."

"But — " Angie said, stopping in midsentence to try to figure this all out " — she's supposed to fall in love with Chris Page. I've got it all planned."

"Well, maybe that'll happen, but I don't think she was thinking about Chris Page much yesterday afternoon."

Mary Ellen pushed open the door to the office of Tarenton High's school newspaper.

"Hi," she said to Ronni Williams, a senior who was editor this year. Ronni was sitting at a big worktable pasting galleys onto the dummy of next week's front page.

"You seen Patrick?" Mary Ellen asked her.

"Darkroom," Ronni said, nodding toward the closed door in the back, the one with a red light over it.

Mary Ellen knocked.

"Yeah?" came Patrick's reedy voice from within.

"It's me. Mary Ellen."

"Oh. Great. Hold on, can you? I'm in the middle of developing. It'll just be a few minutes."

"I'll sit outside here. I've got to study my irregular verbs for French, anyway."

"Uh oh," he said, "I'd better hurry, in that case. Or you'll be asleep by the time I get out."

And, even though it only took him ten minutes or so, she *was* asleep by the time he opened the door.

He put a gentle hand on her shoulder.

Snore.

"Mary Ellen?" he said, bending close to her ear.

"Hmmph?" she sputtered, her eyelids springing suddenly open. She looked down at the little pack of three-by-five cards in her lap and said, "Irregular verbs. They do it to me every time. How am I ever going to pass French if I fall asleep every time I get these cards out?"

"Maybe you should forget passing French and just make a million dollars selling the cards as a sleep aid," he said, folding his lanky frame down next to her so they were sitting side by side on the floor.

She laughed.

"Great idea. Especially since you're on *your* way to becoming a millionaire, going into partnership and everything. Big time." She traced a fingernail around the bleached-out knees of his jeans.

"Well, the partnership depends on Pres."

"I had lunch with him today. I think he's going to do it. If only to spite his folks and Claudia."

"I think she only likes him for his money," Patrick said.

"He's beginning to think so, too. If it's true, it's crummy. And it got me to feeling crummy about the way I treat you. I mean it's not really much different, is it?"

"I'm not sure I understand. You couldn't possibly love me for my money."

"No, it's the other side of the coin. I'm always saying I'm not going to fall in love with you because of your lack of money. It's just as shallow. And just as phony. Because, well, I really *do* already love you."

He turned and looked at her and let his jaw drop.

"Really?"

She nodded. "I'm not sure what to do about it, but admitting it seems like a good first step."

"I'm too stunned to even kiss you," he said.

"Then I'll have to take the initiative, I guess," Mary Ellen said, covering his mouth softly with hers.

"Come on, you guys!" Ronni Williams yelled from the other side of the room. "Are we putting out a paper here, or just steaming up the windows?" Ronni was a very serious person, about everything, but especially about the paper.

"Okay, all right," Patrick shouted back at Ronni, then turned and whispered to Mary Ellen, "Come into the darkroom. I want to show you something."

Inside, hanging from a line by a clothespin, was an eight-by-ten photo of the whole cheerleading squad in full dress, in a pyramid with Olivia on top, pompons and megaphones lined up like a little border in front of them.

"Oh, it's great!" Mary Ellen said.

"It's the best of the bunch I took," he said. "I think it definitely ought to be the one you send on to the competition. If any other school in the region has a squad that looks as good as this, I'd like to see it!"

CHAPTER

12

"We don't need no music,
We don't need no band!
All we need is Tarenton fans,
Jammin' in the stands!"

The squad shouted this one through their megaphones, then punctuated the cheer with a fairly dazzling set of running aerial flips, but nothing could get the small group of Tarenton fans jammin' in the stands by the end of the game at Deep River Tuesday night.

Tarenton had drifted farther and farther behind through the whole final period and finally lost by 26 points. Amid the exuberant hordes of Deep River fans reveling their way out of the gym, the small contingent from Tarenton was sort of sulking its way out to the parking lot.

"This is the hardest time to be a cheerleader," Angie said to Nancy as they got their equipment together. "The fans look at you like, 'There's nothing to cheer about, so what are *you* doing here?' "

"I know," Nancy said, "and I'm already so down myself that suddenly being a cheerleader seems ridiculous. In my lowest moments, I ask myself, Why didn't I join Future Nurses instead?"

"At the same time," Olivia chimed in, "you don't want to let the team down. They already feel rotten enough. And so you keep this stupid smile plastered across your face. I feel like I'm wearing a mask."

"Well, if we have to lose," Walt added, "better at away games than at home. And best of all at weeknight away games like this. That way you only have to lose in front of a few die-hard fans."

"I know," Angie said. "There were so few tonight that each of their gloomy faces is indelibly etched in my memory." She paused, looking toward the door, surprise reshaping her features. "And this isn't one of them."

The object of her surprise was Chris Page, who was trying to get into the Deep River gym, pushing against the tide of people leaving.

"Hi," he said, smiling at Angie.

She found she just couldn't come up with a response to this. Sometimes he simply took her

93

breath away. In between the times when she saw him, she forgot a little how gorgeous he was. And so every time he came around a corner, or through a cafeteria doorway, or into a classroom, she was as astonished as the first time she'd seen him. She was working on getting this under control. Now that she'd just begun to make friends with him, she didn't want to ruin everything by going goony in front of him. Still, standing so close to him, looking up into his outrageously blue eyes, watching him run his fingers through his thick blond hair, breathing in the peppery fragrance of his aftershave, it was hard to feel just friendly.

"I was just passing through the neighborhood and saw the light on and thought I'd stop in and see if anyone wanted a ride back to Tarenton," he said, grinning. "Like maybe you."

"Oh, well, uh, I was planning to go back on the team bus with . . . uh . . . with the other cheerleaders." What she'd really been planning was to get Nancy in a hammerlock and wring out of her what she was up to, who this new guy was — the Hamburger Heaven kisser. A lot of times things seemed to happen so fast around Tarenton High, Angie could hardly keep up with all the subplots.

"Oh," Chris said, clearly disappointed. He hadn't, of course, just been in the neighborhood. Deep River was twenty-five miles away from Tarenton. He'd come out to fetch Angie and she knew it. What she couldn't figure out was why.

Of course, he didn't have many friends here yet. Maybe he was just lonely. And it *would* be nice to ride back with him along the dark highway. Nice and awful at the same time. The problem was that she couldn't let him see that she was beginning to be attracted to him. She didn't want him to think she was like every other girl at Tarenton High. But hiding all that she felt for him required such a huge effort, and it was getting harder all the time.

"I don't have to go with the rest of them," she told him, unable to resist. "Who wants to sit in that smelly old bus, anyhow?"

When they were on their way, the radio playing softly, the heater making it warm and cozy inside the car, he said, "Reach over in the backseat. I brought something for you."

Angie looked and saw a beat-up old manila envelope. She pulled it over the seat and onto her lap. She started to unstick the flap. He reached over and pressed his hand over hers.

"Not now," he said. "Please. After I drop you off. And even then you'd better wait until I'm a few blocks away. In case you laugh really loud."

"Aha! Your poems!" She held the envelope up.

"Shhh," he said, pretending to look suspiciously from side to side. "The car may be bugged. I don't want anyone finding this out. It's my deepest, darkest secret."

"Safe with me," Angie said, crossing her heart

95

and turning the imaginary key to her lips.

He smiled.

"I haven't seen anyone do that since I was a kid."

"Kid stuff is some of the best stuff," she said. "I still skip sometimes when no one's looking. And I can't pass by hopscotch squares on a sidewalk without giving it a shot."

He nodded.

"I know what you mean. I still walk through the middle of puddles. I know I'm too old to still be doing it, but I don't care."

They fell silent for a while. She watched him while he drove through the black night, broken only here and there by lights from a roadside tavern or distant farmhouse. It was interesting getting to look at him this way, when he wasn't aware of it, when he wasn't looking at her.

"You were being serious underneath it all, weren't you?" she asked him. "About the poems? You really are trusting me with something personal and important to you, aren't you?"

He nodded and said, "Yeah. It's kind of a new thing for me. I've hardly ever let anyone in."

"Because it's scary?" she asked.

"You give someone a piece of yourself, you're vulnerable to them. It's easier keeping everybody outside."

"Especially easier when you look like you do," Angie said.

"How do you mean?" he said.

"Well, guys who weigh four hundred pounds

96

and have bad skin have to get people to like them for their inner selves. But you can just drift through the halls a few times and about six girls will fall for you just because you look so cute in your black sweater and faded jeans."

"Boy," he said, then whistled softly. "You really call 'em like you see 'em."

Actually, she couldn't believe she was talking to him this way. Ordinarily she would've been totally tongue-tied. It was moments like these that made her happy he wasn't interested in her. It freed her up to be real with him, in a way she hardly ever could with guys. She became more determined than ever to not think of him as appealing. Maybe if she tried to imagine that he did weigh four hundred pounds and had bad skin, it would be easier.

When he pulled up in front of her house, he shut off the ignition and turned toward her.

"Will you be honest with me about the poems?" he said, gesturing toward the envelope she was holding.

"Yes," she said. "And I'll give you mine as soon as I get up the courage."

"Please don't show them to anyone else," he said.

"Oh, Chris, I wouldn't! I'll even keep them under my mattress so no one in my family finds them."

"Maybe we should rent a vault," he said, laughing at himself. "I mean, do I sound neurotic or what?"

"Poets get to be neurotic," she said. "It comes with the job. Like insurance. So . . ." she was stalling. She didn't want to go. In this pause, she watched as he reached an arm over toward her. Thinking that since they were just friends, he must just want to shake hands, she gave him hers. Instead of shaking it, though, he kissed it softly.

Angie didn't know what to make of this. Maybe guys in California were into old-movie stuff. Like Walt was. That must be it. So, taking this cue, she gave him a little knuckle tap on his jaw and said, "Here's looking at you, kid."

Then she hopped out of the car.

Even though it was late, Chris was starving and he pulled into the Taco Taco on his way home. There was hardly anyone in the place. While he was watching the counter girl take an incredibly long time to put together a Coke and a Super Taco, in came Patrick Henley.

"Chris Page, right?" he said when he got up to the counter.

Chris nodded and said, "Patrick Henley."

"Right. So . . ." he started, then interrupted himself to point at the counter girl. "Boy, she is really slow, isn't she? I think she's putting the lettuce on that taco shred by shred."

"And it's *my* taco," Chris said glumly.

"Maybe this is a new concept. They feel fast food is getting boring, and so they're giving us Slow Food! And just when I'm starving! Starvation is one of the side effects of being in love

98

with a very thin girl. Mary Ellen's always on a diet, never wants to go out for anything to eat after games. And so I find myself wandering through the night, looking for an honest hamburger, a solid taco."

"Same here," Chris said. "I just dropped Angie off. I asked her if she wanted to come along with me, but she said she had to study, and would grab her standard midnight snack — lettuce and a Tab. To me lettuce isn't a snack. Unless it's on top of a taco, of course."

"You seeing Angie Poletti?" Patrick asked.

Chris ran a hand through his hair and thought for a moment.

"Well, that's a tricky question. I've been *seeing* her quite a bit, but I can't seem to make any progress. I've never been so crazy about a girl, but I don't think the feeling's mutual. She's really nice to me, but I'm pretty sure she just thinks of me as a friend. She actually wanted to shake my hand good-night tonight. This isn't a problem I've had too much experience with before. I don't know what's wrong. Does she have another guy she's going with, or something?"

"Not that I know of," Patrick said.

"Then I don't know. Maybe it's my breath. Or maybe you've got different social customs than we have in California. Out there, when you pay as much attention to a girl as I've been paying to Angie, she gets the idea that you're interested in her."

The counter girl was finally done with Chris's

order. Patrick gave her his and then turned back to helping Chris think this through.

"I don't know," he finally said. "I never seem to be able to understand girls very well, but I'd guess Angie would be interested in you. All I can figure is that she thinks you want to be friends and that's all, and so that's the tone she's sticking with. Maybe if you were just really direct with her about this, you could get things on the right track. You know, the sledgehammer-of-love approach."

Chris gave him a question-mark look.

"You know," Patrick explained. "You take her face between your hands and look straight into her eyes and tell her just how you feel about her."

"Did you ever actually use this technique?" Chris asked.

"Yeah, about six months ago. With Mary Ellen."

"And? Did it work?"

"Well, not right away. For the first five months and most of the sixth, she wouldn't have much to do with me. But it must have had a subtle effect because finally yesterday she told me she loves me."

"Boy," Chris said, shaking his head. "Six months."

"Oh, don't think that way. Mary Ellen and I are a special case. With you two, it'll probably work out right away. Really, with love, I think honesty is the sanest policy. Otherwise everybody's always going around confused. Girls are crying in the bathroom, guys are moping around on the basketball court."

"All right, I'll do it," Chris said, picking strands of grated cheese off his taco, and eating them and thinking.

During this pause, Patrick looked first over Chris's shoulder, behind the counter, where the counter girl was still trying to fold his burrito into something like a burrito shape. She was consulting the Taco Taco employee's manual. This was going to take a while.

Then he turned and scanned the sparse, late-night crowd in the restaurant, and was surprised to see Vanessa there. Even more surprised to see that she was in deep conversation with Betty Sims, captain of the cheerleading squad from Tarenton's archrival, Garrison High. Vanessa was passing some papers across the table to her.

He couldn't figure this one out, but knew he'd better pass it on to Mary Ellen.

CHAPTER 13

"'**H**ey, hey, howdy,'" Mary Ellen said, reading from the notebook on her lap, biting the eraser end of her pencil.

"What about if we make it 'Hey, hi, howdy'?" said Angie. "You know, vary the sounds a little."

"You're right, that's good," Mary Ellen said, penciling in the change.

It was Friday afternoon and all four female cheerleaders were sitting around — or, rather, flopped around, in various positions on the bed and floor of Nancy's bedroom. Ardith Engborg had given the squad the assignment of coming up with a sensational opening cheer for the competition and the six of them had decided that the girls would come up with the words, then Walt and Pres would put moves to them.

102

"So what've we got now, Mary Ellen?" Olivia asked. "Can you read through the whole thing?"

"Sure —

> Hey, hi, howdy,
> Tarenton — get rowdy!
> Hey, hi, hello,
> Come on, Wolves, let's go!"

"Nice," Angie said. "Short and sweet, but it ought to give the guys enough to work with."

"I think it's a great cheer," Nancy said. "Hey, why don't I run downstairs and get us some soda and chips? As long as we're all here and finished working, we might as well hang out for a while." She leaped off her brass bed with its soft down comforter and bounded downstairs.

Olivia looked at her watch.

"I've got a date with Walt at seven. It's almost five now. Well, I guess that leaves me enough time for a little gossip."

"Well, as long as you're here, we might as well start with you," Mary Ellen teased. "That way you can't accuse us of talking behind your back. So come on, tell us how Walt's kissing lessons are going."

"Oh," Olivia said, blushing so hard she took one of Nancy's pillows and pressed her face into it so the others couldn't see.

"Come on, Livvy!" Angie said, pulling the pillow away, and then giving Olivia a light thump with it to prod her into talking. "Spill the beans.

We're your friends. You *have* to tell us the juicy details. It's what friendship's all about. It's repayment for all the hours we've spent listening to your problems."

"Oh, all right," Olivia conceded. "He's terrific."

"What do you mean?" Mary Ellen said. "I thought the reason for the lessons was that he *wasn't* terrific."

"Well, the lessons are working, I guess. Or else he's just a quick learner."

"Who's a quick learner? What lessons?" Nancy said, coming back into the room with a six-pack of root beer cans dangling from one hand, a bag of chips from the other. She pulled off some cans and passed them around.

"Walt's kissing tutorial," Mary Ellen said. "Apparently he's getting all A's."

"Must be rough on you two," Nancy said with fake sympathy, "all these squad workouts, and then on top of it, having to put in hours on your kissing. You must be exhausted."

"Argh!" Olivia wailed. "Give me back my pillow so I can hide! Pick on Nancy for a while. The way it looked at Hamburger Heaven, she's into college-level kissing — and we don't even know who the tutor is!"

"Nancy!" Mary Ellen said. "You've been holding out on us! How could you? Who is he?"

"Oh. Just a friend."

"I never kissed 'just a friend' like that," Olivia interjected.

"His name's Greg Connors. He's a sophomore at the J.C. in Hillsborough. He's in the swim program where I'm helping out. You can meet him if you want. He's coming by in an hour or so. We're going to the Bijou. They've got a marathon night of awful horror movies from the past. *Creature from the Black Lagoon. I Was a Teen-Age Werewolf. The Slime That Ate Cleveland.* We thought it'd be fun to go."

"Boy," Angie said. "Here I was, doing all this engineering to get you together with Chris Page, and there you were, off on your own, going after this college guy."

"Chris Page isn't interested in me," Nancy said, then took a sip of root beer before going on. "He's got someone else in mind."

"Who?" Olivia asked.

"Welllll," Nancy said, stretching out the suspense, "she's someone we all know for her cute looks and generous heart and great lasagna. Someone sitting right here in this room."

"Thanks for that description," Angie said, "but you're still crazy. Chris and I are just good friends."

"There seems to be a lot of that going around," Mary Ellen said, tossing back her long blonde hair and laughing. "I myself am tired of pretending to friendship. I've confessed true love to Patrick Henley, garbageman of my dreams."

"No!" Nancy said, pulling a couple of chips out of the bag and passing it along to Olivia. "But what about your career? What about New York?"

"I don't know. Maybe I'll have to rethink my plans. Maybe Patrick and I can work out some sort of compromise. But whatever, I just knew I had to tell him. I had to be honest. I was beginning to feel like one of those coy belles in old movies about the South. You know, dangling a suitor along forever, fluttering my fan and saying I just don't know how I feel about him." She stretched out on the rug next to Nancy's bed and said, "I feel a whole lot better since I told him."

"Boy, a lot's been happening lately," Olivia said. "This is the juiciest gossip session I've had in months. And we didn't even get to Vanessa."

"I heard you two were despicable to her," Nancy said. "And I innocently told her to take your advice, whatever it was, so now she probably hates me, too. We'd better keep an eye out. She's bound to be deep into a revenge fantasy by now."

From outside the front window came the honk of a car horn. Nancy leaped up and went over to look.

"Oh good! It's Greg! He's early. Now you can all meet him."

They all hopped up and ran down the carpeted stairs and out onto Nancy's sidewalk — just in time to see Greg hoisting himself, both hands grasping onto the roof of the car, out into his wheelchair.

He looked up and saw he was under observation by four girls, three of whom he didn't know and who were standing there with mouths open in surprise. This got him so flustered that his pale, freckled face went nearly as red as his hair.

Too late, Nancy realized what a terrible mistake she'd made. If she was going to introduce Greg to her friends, why hadn't she been thoughtful enough to do it in a situation where he would've been more comfortable?

Then, to make things even worse, if that was possible, suddenly her parents were there, too, standing on the front steps, surveying the whole scene. Nancy turned back to Greg and threw her hands up. The situation had so quickly gone into the realm of the absurd that there was nothing to do but make a joke out of it.

"The band's about to arrive any minute now," she said to him, grinning weakly. Then, so he wouldn't have to sit there any longer, looking like he was facing a firing squad, she went over and stood behind his chair.

"Everybody, this is Greg Connors. Thanks to my great coaching, this guy may just place in the regional Special Athletics swim meet."

The other girls all clustered around Greg to say hi. Nancy's parents, though, stayed up on the front steps.

Why are they doing this? Nancy thought. They're watching this like it's something happening on TV.

"Mom. Dad. My friend, Greg," she said, trying to bring them in. But all they did was say hi, and then disappear back into the house. She couldn't tell if they were being standoffish, or if they just wanted to get out of the way so they wouldn't seem like chaperones. Usually Nancy got along great with her parents. They hardly ever came down hard on her. She didn't know what they'd say, though, about her having a boyfriend who got around on wheels instead of feet. She hadn't mentioned Greg yet, though, and they couldn't know if he was just a friend, or more. How could they, when Nancy didn't know herself?

Even with them back in the house, the situation in the driveway wasn't terrifically comfortable. Nancy could tell that her friends were having trouble trying to talk to Greg, working overtime trying not to mention the obvious. She wanted to tell them it was all right, that Greg realized he was sitting in a wheelchair, that they didn't have to tiptoe around the subject. But she was afraid that saying something would just make them feel more awkward and Greg, more uncomfortable.

And so she just stood there, watching her friends trying too hard to be nice.

"Nancy says you go to the J.C. in Hillsborough," Mary Ellen said.

"Yeah, I'm in my second year," Greg said, wheeling back and forth slightly. Nancy had noticed that he did this when he was nervous. "I'll go to State next year."

"Do you live at home?" Angie said.

"Do you have brothers and sisters?" Olivia added.

What is this — Twenty Questions? Nancy thought. They're treating him like he's a foreign exchange student or an alien from outer space — like he's really different. It's my fault. I should've told them more about him before he got here. It's an unfair burden to put on him.

She was beginning to see that being with Greg in real life was going to be more complicated than being with him in the pool.

"Hey," she told her friends now, "if Greg and I are going to make the movie, we have to split pretty soon."

She ran up to get a jacket, and by the time she came back down, the other girls were getting into Angie's old Ford, a rusted-out wreck painted pink with a black convertible top. Angie called it the Good & Plenty. This car was a weird source of pride to her. It had been in her family for years, passed along from cousin to nephew and so on. It was kind of a family joke to try to keep it running. She sat behind the wheel now, trying to start it, but the ignition wasn't catching.

"Out and about!" she told Mary Ellen and Olivia, who were used to this. They hopped out and, grunting and groaning, pushed it the few feet necessary to get the engine to kick over. Angie gunned it in neutral while they hopped back in, and they were off, waving out the windows at Nancy and Greg.

She turned to see him looking unusually glum. "That's one of the parts I hate most," he said.

"Meeting new people?"

"No. When something comes up where guys are expected to do some 'guy' thing, and I just have to sit here like a potato."

"Oh, I wouldn't worry about that," she told him, sitting down on the front fender of his car, facing him. "It probably makes you less macho."

"Actually, I think I'm more macho since the accident. Before, I didn't have to prove anything. Now I feel like I've got to prove everything."

"Not to me," she said.

"Especially to you," he said.

Suddenly the conversation was making her nervous. She felt the need to lighten it up.

"Hey, I thought you were taking me to some horror movies," she said, jumping down off the hood and tickling him in the ribs. "Come on. I'm ready to be scared!"

They wound up watching — or at least sitting and whispering and kissing through — three old horror pictures. It was past one when Greg dropped Nancy off at her house. She was surprised to see the living room lights still on. Usually her parents just left the porch light and front hall lamp on, so she could find her way in.

"Uh oh," she said to Greg as she was getting out of the car, "I think I'm being awaited by the parental units."

110

"Is this too late for you to be getting in?"

"Not usually."

"Do you think it's about me?"

She debated whether to lie or not, and decided to be honest.

"Probably," she said. "Don't worry, though. I'll handle it."

"I won't come around anymore if it's going to cause a lot of problems."

"Don't be silly," she said, coming around to his side, leaning in through the open window and kissing him. "See you Sunday. And *on time*. Now that the tryouts are getting close, the coach has to get tough."

"Yes ma'am!" Greg said, saluting before he backed down the driveway.

Nancy came in the house, hung her jacket on the bentwood coat tree, and peeked into the living room on her way up the stairs. Both of her parents were there — her father stretched out on the sofa in front of the fireplace, her mom in the wing chair by the window. They were watching an old Ingrid Bergman movie on TV. Maybe she could just slip by, up the stairs to her room.

"Nancy!" came her father's voice before she was halfway up. "Can we see you for a minute?"

"Well, I'm really tired."

"Just for a minute," her mother said.

She came in and sat in the easy chair opposite the sofa.

"It's pretty late," her father said, sitting up

and clicking off the TV. A bad sign.

"I've been in this late lots of times. It's a Friday night, after all."

"Where'd you go?" her mother asked.

"To the Bijou. I think I told you. To see the horror festival."

"It's nice of you to take your friend . . ." her father started.

"Greg," Nancy interjected.

"Greg. Nice of you to take such an interest in him — I mean beyond the swimming."

"Nice of him to take an interest in *me*," Nancy said, hearing the edge in her voice. Usually she and her parents were pretty tuned in to each other. It wasn't like them to grill her like this.

She was trying to figure what was behind all this when her mother said, "I ran into Ann Peterson this afternoon at the supermarket and she mentioned seeing you the other day."

"Oh," Nancy said, trying to sound uninterested in this conversation.

"Yes, last Sunday afternoon. She was bringing Billy back from soccer practice and they stopped off at Hamburger Heaven."

"Boy!" Nancy sputtered, and then began to laugh in spite of the apparent seriousness of the situation. "It looks like if I live to be ninety, I won't live down that kiss. Everybody in Tarenton must've just happened to be driving by the old HH Sunday afternoon."

"Well, the point isn't that you were kissing in the Hamburger Heaven," her father said, "although you might show a little more restraint in public. The point is that this is apparently a romance between you and . . . Greg, not just swimming lessons."

"So?" Nancy said.

"Well, honey," her mother said, her tone shifting from tense to concerned, "have you thought of all the problems involved?"

"Mom. All I've done with him is kiss at the Hamburger Heaven and sit through three terrible monster pictures. We haven't signed any contracts in blood. We're not running off to a wedding chapel."

"We're not hassling you, Nance," her father said. "We just want to keep in touch."

"But you *are* hassling me," Nancy said defensively. "And what if I did fall in love with Greg and marry him and live happily ever after in our wheelchair-accessible house? So, it would be harder. Big deal. Maybe he's worth it." She could tell she was raising her voice, but she felt overpowered by the need to defend Greg. "He's one of the most courageous people I've ever met. He's determined not to let his accident stop him from living. I've seen Pres more frustrated when his Porsche is in the shop for a couple of days than I've ever seen Greg over the fact that he'll never walk again. Most of the time I forget he's got a handicap. All I see is a funny, smart, sensitive, deep person. And if I want to fall in love with him — it's *my* business!"

"And if you do, we'll be behind you one-hundred percent, as usual," her father said. But Nancy didn't really hear him. She was already stomping upstairs and into her room, slamming the door so hard that her old Mrs. Bunny doll toppled off its shelf onto her head. Somehow this was just the last straw, and sent her facedown on her bed, sobbing.

CHAPTER

14

Angie was baby-sitting for the Fiorello kids — Laurie and Sarah — who were such terrors that she was thinking of charging the Fiorellos double the usual rate. Tonight, while she was in the bathroom, cleaning up the mess of their shaving-cream fight, the girls dumped five boxes of cereal on the kitchen floor so they could "skate" around on it in their shoes. Angie thought that, even though they were only five and seven, the Fiorello girls could probably get full-time work with a wrecking company.

When she'd finally gotten them to bed and then, an hour later, gotten them to stop singing every song they had learned in nursery school and day camp and kindergarten, Angie flopped down on the sofa in the family room and opened the envelope of Chris's poems. She'd read them a dozen times now, and thought they were really good. One, though, was her special favorite:

> *Seafoam mornings blur into*
> *blue afternoons.*
> *Black beach nights erase themselves*
> *as I sleep, and wake to watch dawn*
>   *covering you.*

It was clear he'd written this one back in California, a place she'd never seen, and about a girl she didn't know. Somehow none of that mattered. The poem was so vivid that she could imagine herself there on that beach with him, could imagine herself as the girl he wrote this about.

She was pulled out of this drifting reverie by a strong wind rushing through the house. Off in the distance there was a flash of lightning.

"Uh oh," Angie said. She hated thunderstorms. Especially when she was alone. Double especially when she was baby-sitting.

She ran through the house, closing all the windows, then came back down to the family room and called Mary Ellen.

"Oh, great," Angie said when Mary Ellen answered on the other end.

"Where are you?" Mary Ellen asked. "I tried to call, but your brother Andrew said you were out. And why is it so great to be talking to me? I mean I know I'm your best friend, but you don't usually appreciate me so noticeably."

"It's great to be talking to you because I'm at the Fiorellos' and a huge storm is coming up and every time it storms when I'm baby-sitting, I think of all those movies where the psychopath comes looking for the baby-sitter."

"Wooowooowooo," Mary Ellen sang in a ghost voice.

"Stop it," Angie said. "You're supposed to be calming me down, not getting me more worked up."

"Angie, there's nothing to worry about. At least not from psychopaths. From the Fiorello girls, maybe, but not from psychopaths. You don't look enough like Jamie Lee Curtis."

"Oh, thanks," Angie said sarcastically.

"You're a different type. What did the little darlings do tonight?"

"Well, first we had a shaving-cream war, then some soft-shoe dancing on spilled Wheaties, then a sing-along. I'm just hoping the storm doesn't wake them up. They'll put on their ghost suits and pop out of closets at me. They know I'm afraid of the thunder and lightning. Do you think the Fiorello kids are demonically possessed?"

"If they are, then you definitely ought to ask Mrs. Fiorello for that raise. I say, as a rule of thumb, a dollar an hour extra for possessed children. Say, did you check the basement?"

"The basement? No. Why?"

"Well, that's where the psychopath was hiding in one of those movies I saw."

117

"Melon!" Angie shrieked. "I'll talk to you later. I've got to go check the basement."

She ran to the kitchen, where the steps to the basement were, but couldn't bring herself to open the door. Basements, even without psychopaths lurking in them, were just too scary. Even an ordinary basement could have spiders and mice. Ugh. Just the thought was enough to keep her standing right where she was. The boldest step she could take was to reach out and push in the button in the center of the doorknob. Now whatever was down there would have to unlock the door before it could get to her.

As she stood looking nervously at the closed basement door, standing very still so she could hear footsteps if there were any, the phone rang loudly, causing her to jump.

Mary Ellen, she thought, calling back to apologize for scaring me.

She picked up the receiver on the kitchen wall phone and shouted into it, "Well, you ought to be sorry!"

"Huh? What for?"

The voice on the other end definitely wasn't Mary Ellen's. It was definitely a guy's.

"Oh. Sorry," Angie said. "Who is this?"

"Chris."

"Chris Page?"

"You have so many Chrises calling you that you can't keep us all apart?" he teased. "I called your house and your mom gave me this number.

You're over on Peartree Lane," he said. "That's the next street over from me."

Just then a huge clap of thunder, followed almost immediately by a vicious crack of lightning, broke through the sky.

"Eeeeee!" Angie squealed.

"You okay?" Chris said.

"It's just the storm. I'm a wimp about them. So it's a good time for you to call. Maybe you can talk some sense into me."

"Have you got the right person. You happen to be talking to someone who did his seventh-grade science-fair project on rain. I'll tell you all about cumulus clouds and atmospheric electricity. I'll boil the whole thing down to facts so boring they'll put you to sleep."

"Won't do any good," Angie said woefully. "As soon as the next crack of thunder comes, I'll be reduced to a gibbering blob of putty again. It's really pitiful."

"Well," Chris said, "maybe if I change the subject. You know, distract you. I'll tell you what I called to tell you in the first place."

"What's that?" Angie asked.

"Well, you see, I've been having this problem for a couple of weeks now. There's this girl here in Tarenton I'm crazy about. I think she likes me, but every time I try to get close to her, she acts like we're in the same coin-collecting club or something. You know, nice, but strictly buddy-buddy. So I asked a couple of her friends what to do and they said, Go for it, tell her straight out how you feel. Don't leave an inch of room for confusion or misinterpretation. What do you think?"

"I think it's a good idea."

"All right then, I'll do it. Angie, I'm crazy about you."

Just then another huge crackling wave of lightning, coupled with a gigantic clap of thunder, crashed through the night sky. It also glitched the phone line.

"What?" Angie shouted into the receiver. "I can't hear you."

"I said I think you're the most wonderful girl I've ever met. I think I'm falling in love with you."

Although there was no lightning or thunder now, Angie said, "We must still have a terrible connection. You can't have just said what I thought you said."

"Okay," Chris said. "I'm going to hang up and try for a better connection."

Angie put the receiver back in its cradle and then just sat on the kitchen stool next to the phone waiting for it to ring again. But it didn't. She waited and waited, for maybe five minutes before she gave up and wandered into the living room. By now the commotion outside had stopped and settled into just a lot of rain. It seemed to be pouring in solid sheets from the sky. This part of storms didn't scare her, so she was free to stand and watch the rain and wonder where Chris Page had disappeared to, and if she'd heard him right.

She didn't have to wonder long. As she stood looking out the front window, suddenly there he was, running full-tilt across the street, over the sidewalk and up the lawn, his blond hair curled against his head by the driving rain.

Angie ran to the front door and unlocked it and threw it open. For a moment, they stood on opposite sides of the threshold, just looking at each other. Chris was the one to speak first.

"I thought maybe we could make a better connection in person," he said, rain dripping from his long lashes, his hair, nose, and chin, and sliding off his slicker onto the porch floor. "If I stand here and tell you I'm falling in love with you, you'll have to hear me."

"Oh, Chris," Angie said.

"You're not going to tell me I'm all wet," Chris punned.

Angie smiled and said, "Oh, no."

And let herself be pulled — forgetting about the rain — out onto the front porch, into his arms and his kiss. She stood there for several long, wonderful moments, holding him and being held before a certain sound brought her back to the real world. It was the sound of the gentle but firm shutting and locking of a door. The front door.

She looked up quickly and saw she was right. And she knew where to look next — through the window. Standing there in the warm, dry living room were Laurie and Sarah Fiorello, giggling in their nightgowns. Laurie, the older sister, was motioning for Angie to press her ear to the window so they could tell her something.

"Mommy and Daddy are sure going to be surprised when they come home and find you outside," she said smugly, following little Sarah off to find some mischief to get into.

"Argh!" Angie said, pounding on the window frame with her fist. Then she looked at Chris and, seeing the absurdity of the situation, collapsed with him into a heap of laughter.

CHAPTER 15

Nancy had come to really love her Sunday mornings at the pool. Greg was a big part of it, of course, but not all of it. In these past couple of years that she hadn't been swimming, she'd forgotten how much she loved the feel of gliding through water, the light tension that came with testing herself against the clock. These Sundays were bringing all this back to her. Most times now, she came early and put in a mile of her own before the handicapped workout began.

Swimming gave her time of her own to just think. Back and forth, putting in her laps, away from the voices of her parents and teachers and friends, she could get into a place she thought of as Deep Thought. And she needed time there these days. She had a lot of thought to get deep about.

Everything suddenly seemed so complicated. She still cried every night in bed about Ben. Why did he have to die? No one close to her had ever died before. His death had opened up a whole bunch of thoughts. About other people in her life dying. About her own mortality. All of these thoughts were depressing.

And then meeting Greg had thrown a whole other set of thoughts into the mix. At first he had just added to the depression. First someone she cared about had died a terrible, stupid, accidental death. Now she cared about someone who'd had to go through a terrible, stupid accident.

But then getting to know Greg better, she started seeing how his inner strength made him as complete as people with all their limbs still working.

But why couldn't her parents see this? Or her friends? In the days since they'd met Greg, they hadn't said anything about him, which was almost worse. She knew what their silence meant — that they thought it was sad or pathetic that she was in love with a paraplegic.

Which brought her to the dumbest problem of all. She felt that, just to spite them all, she should fall in love with Greg. The problem was that she couldn't. And it didn't have to do with him being in a wheelchair. She admired him and liked him a lot. And liked the way he looked and kissed a double lot. But he and she were so different. She was Jewish and he was Catholic. She wanted a career and he was looking for a girl who wanted to get married and raise a big family. Her idea of travel was Paris, his was fishing up at Otter Lake. It had gotten so they just laughed at how they had such different ideas on everything.

A further problem was that these differences didn't seem to bother Greg at all. He thought somehow they'd resolve them all eventually. She was pretty sure he was in love with her.

All in all, the situation seemed like such a gigantic mess that she figured she'd need to swim about a hundred miles before she could get enough Deep Thought time to sort it all out.

When she had done maybe three quarters of a mile, she noticed that Eric Campbell was standing at the end of her lane. He motioned to her as she was pulling out of her flip turn and could see him. She finished out the lap, then came up at his feet and pulled off her goggles and cap so she could see and hear him.

"Got a minute before the workout starts?" he asked. She nodded and pulled herself out. He didn't wait for her, just walked back to the office, which was windowed off at the end of the pool. Following him, Nancy thought, if only he weren't so brusque all the time, he'd be kind of a neat guy.

From the beginning she had noticed how much Eric looked like Mel Gibson, with his short, stand-up black hair and dark eyes and tightly muscled body. But he was always so abrupt and official acting that it was impossible to consider him sexy. Actually, Nancy had found it impossible to consider him even friendly. She was surprised he wanted to talk to her now. Probably about training schedules.

She dried off with her towel as she walked into the office. He was sitting on the corner of the desk in his red-, white-, and blue-striped racing suit and a navy hooded sweatshirt, his ever-present whistle on a lanyard around his neck.

He probably sleeps with that thing on, Nancy thought.

"It's about Greg," he said.

"His training schedule?" Nancy asked, rubbing the water out of her hair with the towel.

"No, his feelings about you."

"Boy, Eric, as usual, you don't waste words. Well, what about it? You think hugging me is bad for his pectoral muscles or something?" Ordinarily she would have been embarrassed at a conversation this personal, but at the moment she just thought Eric was way out of line, and was angry at the way he'd just summoned her in here and launched in on this.

"I think the whole business is more than he can handle at the moment," Eric went on.

"Oh, you do, do you?" Nancy said huffily. "And where, may I ask, did you get that idea?"

"From him," Eric said.

"Oh," Nancy said, and sat down in the chair

126

opposite the desk. "You mean he complained to you about me or something?"

"Oh, no. And he'd kill me in cold blood if he knew I was talking to you about this. Greg's wild about you. That's the problem. It's got him scared. The thing is, the guy's been through so many major changes in the past year or two. I gather he used to be a pretty big lady killer before his accident. Since then, though, he hasn't been interested in anyone. Until you. I think it took someone he was really nuts about to make him fall, and now that he has, he's seeing all the complications a relationship would bring and he just can't deal with it all. He's scared to tell you himself. I'm sure he came to me partly because he figured I talk so little I'd never find all the words to tell you."

"But you did, didn't you?" Nancy said. "Honestly, Eric, I think that was the most words I've ever heard you string together at one time."

For a long moment the two of them just sat there in the office. Then Nancy started shaking her head and laughing softly to herself.

"What?" Eric said.

"Well, this is about the craziest situation I've ever been in. Nobody wants me to be in love with Greg, so I've been pretending that I am — to show them, and to not hurt Greg. Who now turns out to not want to be in love with me but is too scared to tell me."

Eric started laughing along with her.

"Oh, no! Eric Campbell actually laughs sometime! This is too many revelations of your true character for one day."

He smiled at her.

"So. What're you going to do?" he asked her.

She shook her head.

"I'm not sure," she said. "I think I'd better have a talk with Greg. I won't mention that you and I talked. He and I are usually pretty good at being straight with each other, though, so we should be able to get out of this soap opera."

She stood and picked up her towel and cap and goggles and started out of the office. When she got to the door, she turned back and said to Eric over her shoulder, "Hey, thanks."

He nodded, back to his usual silent mode, then thought a moment and said, "You're crossing over a little. On your freestyle. I was watching."

Nancy shook her head in amazement.

"Always the coach," she said and went out to the pool where the handicapped swimmers were beginning to file in.

CHAPTER

Within a week, Pres and Patrick had shaken hands on their partnership, and put a down payment on the old bread truck Patrick had found at Big Al's Ace Used Cars & Trucks.

Pres decided not to tell his father about H & T's TLC Moving, or about cleaning out his savings account to start it. Not just yet, anyway. His plan was to hold off until he could show his dad how much money he could make in the moving business. For the time being, they would park the truck at Patrick's.

Their first job was Sunday. Patrick's cousin Sue was getting married and she and her boyfriend were merging their apartments. So it was a double job. They enlisted Walt to help out.

Angie was there at the time and overheard. She wanted to help, too.

"It'd be a good change from baby-sitting. The Fiorello kids are getting to be hazardous to my mental health."

"Well, uh," Pres said, "it's going to be a lot of heavy lifting. You know, guys' work."

Angie's response to this was to lift Pres up into the air, holding him like a baby.

"You mean like this?" she said.

"Okay, okay," Pres said as she put him back down. "I get your point."

Sunday turned out — luckily for Pres and Patrick — to be one of the first really nice days of early spring. Sunny and mild. Everything else about this first move that could go wrong, though, did.

First of all, the fan belt on Big Al's truck snapped on the way to Sue's apartment. This slowed things down for half an hour while they stopped and got a replacement.

As it turned out, they needn't have worried about being late as Sue, the classic bride in a dither, had hardly even started to pack. When they got there, she was sitting on her floor, in the middle of stacks of unpacked books and kitchenware, trying to wrap a large houseplant in newspaper.

"I think we can take that as is," Patrick assured her. "Why don't you get on with your real packing and we'll start taking the furniture down."

Walt stayed there with her to help her pack and organize the move. Pres, Patrick, and Angie started hauling chairs and tables down the three winding flights of stairs.

By the time they had the truck filled up, Pres had a bruised shin from the bed in the convertible sofa falling out on him when they tipped it over. Angie had dropped Sue's huge piggy bank full of pennies on her foot and was limping. Patrick had scraped his leg putting it through the slats on the stair railing while hauling an easy chair down.

"Looks like we've got a few tricks of the trade to learn," Pres said to the others as they headed over to Sue's.

Her boyfriend Eddie's place was worse. He turned out to be a collector of old blacksmith stuff. In addition to a dozen sets of bellows and boxes and boxes of horseshoes, he had seven anvils for them to move. All three apartments — Sue's and Eddie's and their new place — were on third floors, and so there were miles of stairs at every phase of the move.

And then, about three in the afternoon, when they had just brought Eddie's stuff to the new apartment, the "nice" fell out of the bottom of the nice spring day and it started to rain.

Patrick slapped his forehead in disbelief.

"This is like a bad joke."

As if to confirm this statement, a sleek blue

Mercedes sports coupe pulled around the corner. Claudia. She slowed as she rolled past the four movers.

"Nice work if you can get it, eh?" she said, grinning sarcastically, then rolled up her window and peeled off. Pres stood there steaming until Patrick snapped him back to the hard reality of the moment.

"If this stuff gets soaked, we're ruined. We'd better call in the troops. I'll get on the phone to Mary Ellen. She can round everybody up."

Nancy was sitting out in front of her house in Greg's car. It was just starting to rain.

"Thanks for all the work you've been putting in with me," Greg said.

"It's been fun. You know, when I started working in the program, I was in pretty terrible shape."

"About Ben."

"Yes. I could hardly think of anything else. I really couldn't see the point to anything. I felt so powerless. Working with you has turned me around, though. I really feel I've done something worthwhile. I think that if you win at the regionals, it'll be partly because of me. And that's given me the boost I needed. So if anyone's done anyone a favor, it's you. By letting me help you, you've bailed me out."

"This sounds like a farewell speech," he said.

"Oh, no. We've got lots more work to do.

Now that I'm creating a winner, I want to stick around and see him win."

"And there's not another coach I'd rather have. Honestly."

"Sounds like there's a silent 'but' at the end of that sentence," she said.

"Well, it's about at the show, and at Hamburger Heaven."

"I'm too big an eater and you can't afford to take me out again," she said, trying to lighten things up.

"No," he said, still serious.

"Hey," Nancy said, putting her hand over his. "I understand."

"But how can you? I haven't even begun to explain."

"Some things don't need explaining. Those were special moments. Ones I'll never forget. I've never ever been kissed quite like that. And part of its specialness was that it happened between two people who really care about each other. But kissing isn't the whole thing. Neither is swimming. And everything else about us is too different."

"I know," he said, and then took her hand. "You know, the weird thing is that even though I know this can't happen — at least not now — I want to be able to think it could happen, that if the timing were better and we could get over the differences, that you *would* love me. That the obvious problem wouldn't stand in the way."

"Oh, Greg," Nancy said, squeezing his hand back. "You know it wouldn't. I'm a very independent person. I don't care much what other people think. I follow my own heart. And if it had led me to you, I wouldn't let those wheels of yours stand in the way."

He smiled and let go of her hand and reached out and brushed her long dark hair back off her face.

"You're quite a girl, Nancy," he said. "And one heck of a coach."

"But I'm tough. I want you to do *daily* workouts this week!"

His eyes lit up with laughter and Nancy was wondering whether she should give in to the impulse she was feeling to kiss him one more time, when her thoughts were pierced by a call from her mother.

"Nancy!" she shouted out the front door. "Telephone! It's Mary Ellen! Something about helping with a move."

And so Nancy came. And picked up Olivia on the way. And by four the entire cheerleading squad was there pitching in, lugging Eddie's anvils up three flights and reassembling Sue's bookshelves and arranging her plants in by the windows. By seven they were done and utterly exhausted, and extremely happy to see Greg pull up in his car, shouting out the window, "Pizza delivery! I've got pizzas and Cokes if anyone wants 'em!"

Nancy ran over.

"I don't care if we aren't in love," she said, leaning in through his car window, "I'm going to get that kiss I missed earlier." And she did.

Pres and Patrick waited on the front steps for Sue and Eddie to write them a check.

"Next time, we'll have to set it up so we're paid by the hour, not by the job," Patrick said. "I can see this is a lot different than garbage collecting, where you can pretty much gauge how long it will take you. Here you've got to factor in too many other variables."

"I can see that," Pres said ruefully. "After we pay everybody and reimburse Greg for the pizzas, I figure you and I will each make about fifty-six cents on this move. Somehow I don't think that'll impress my dad with what a great businessman I am on my own."

"We'll get smarter as we go along," Patrick reassured him.

"And better," Pres added. "I was thinking we should probably sell customers our own boxes. That way they'd all be the same size and we could stack them so much more easily. Today I felt like every load was bowling balls and bird cages."

"Hey, you guys want to get in on this pizza, or what?" It was Mary Ellen, bearing a large, flat white box. Pres took three slices. Patrick took the rest — and Mary Ellen — and brought her up to the roof garden for a little talk.

"So," he said, "if you love me like you say you

do, does that mean you're going to stay here and help me scour out the garbage truck every night?"

"Oh no. You don't really do that, do you?" she said, looking as if she was not going to be able to eat her pizza.

"No," he said, laughing. "Just testing the limits of this love. But really, what does it mean?"

"I don't know. I guess it means I'm reconsidering leaving," she said, grabbing onto the toes of his shoes. Patrick's big feet were something she had always loved about him. Now that she had told him she loved him, she could grab onto them any time she wanted. Maybe this was worth giving up New York for.

"Or maybe I could go away with you."

"You'd do that?"

"Well, if you're willing to reconsider, I ought to be, too. We don't have to decide anything right now. We've got time to think about options. Do you want another slice, or should I finish this off?"

"Oh, Patrick," she said and sighed. "Maybe I shouldn't think about a future with you. You eat so much. How would we ever make enough to feed you? I'd have to work two jobs. Remember when we went to the Taco Taco and you ate six super burritos?"

He laughed at the memory, and then took a long drink of Coke, then almost spit it out. Instead he swallowed hard and said, "The Taco

Taco. I almost forgot. The other night I was there, getting a little late-night snack. Only one super burrito. Honest. Anyway, I ran into the new guy, Chris Page. We were talking for a while and so I was distracted, but then finally I noticed an unusual twosome in one of the back booths. Vanessa Barlow and Betty Sims — you know, the Garrison cheerleading captain? What could they possibly have to talk about? And how could they even know each other? I couldn't figure out what was up, but I thought I'd better tell you."

"Well, let's see. Vanessa's furious with me and Livvy for pulling that Vassar stunt."

Patrick nodded.

"And she already hates all cheerleaders, anyway."

He nodded again.

"And she knows about the tri-state cheerleading competition. And she knows we're working on these new secret cheers to blast everybody else out of the water."

"Yeah?"

"Well, wouldn't it be possible for her to get hold of those cheers somehow and sell them to the enemy?"

"She *wouldn't*," Patrick said.

"Of course she would," Mary Ellen said. "Would and *is*! Come on, Patrick! We've got to tell the others, and quick! There's no time to waste. That competition's only a week away!"

CHAPTER

17

The headlights from the various cars, trucks, and bikes of the six cheerleaders swept over the front lawn of the little bungalow on Walnut Street where Ardith Engborg lived.

Pres and Angie, Walt and Olivia, and Nancy and Mary Ellen raced up to the front porch, getting there almost simultaneously. They stopped and caught their breath. Ardith had her windows open and the strains of the Notre Dame fight song wafted out from inside. The six of them passed a look among themselves. Any time any of them had ever called or visited Ardith, there was either a game of some kind on the TV, or one of her fight-song collection records on the stereo. Sports and cheering them on were Ardith's main interests in life.

They were glad to find her in, but if she hadn't been, they would have camped out on her porch until she came home. If it had been four in the morning, they would've woken her up. This was too important to keep until school tomorrow. They knew Ardith would want to know right away.

Mary Ellen, wordlessly assuming her authority as squad captain, pressed the doorbell. Ardith appeared almost immediately. She was clearly surprised to see her entire squad on the doorstep. She quickly picked up from their expressions that this wasn't a social call, that something serious was wrong.

She opened the door and motioned for them to follow her inside. When they all got to the living room, she turned down the record and looked at them questioningly.

"It's Vanessa," Mary Ellen said. "Patrick saw her deep in conversation with Betty Sims the other night at Taco Taco. She was passing her some papers. We figure she's getting hold of our new cheers somehow — spying at practices, probably — and passing them along. To try to sabotage us at the competition. Garrison will get their turn before us, alphabetically, and so will always beat us to the punch with our own cheers. We'll just have to concede."

"A truly despicable trick," Ardith said, nodding as she thought it through. "Good thing you found out in time."

"But *is* it in time?" Angie moaned. "There's less than a week until the competition! What can we possibly do now?"

Ardith sat down on the arm of her sofa to gather her thoughts. The others stood waiting, looking around at the walls, which were decorated with pennants from all the high school teams in the area. On the mantel of the fireplace stood two red Tarenton megaphones, and over the doorway hung a cluster of pompons.

Finally Ardith came out of her thoughts and looked around at all of them, then said, "We're going to have to work up a totally new program."

"But how can we?" Walt said. "The program we have now took us over a month to put together."

"Oh, and they're such great cheers," Olivia said, a note of loss in her voice.

"Well, they're not great anymore," Ardith said crisply. "Every single one of them is probably in the hands of the Garrison squad right at this moment. Which makes them worthless currency to us."

"But not to Garrison," Pres mused.

"You're right, Pres," Ardith said. "Garrison could make very good use of those cheers. Technically and acrobatically, Garrison is a terrific squad. Their weakness has always been in their cheers. And it's always been one of our strengths.

So now Vanessa Barlow has not only given Garrison a chance to humiliate us, she's given them a real shot at the championship."

"What a troll," Angie said. "How could she? Can I have permission to go over and give her a punch in the nose?"

"Forget about Vanessa," Ardith cautioned. "We don't have time to worry about her now. I don't want any of your energy siphoned off into revenge. She'll get her comeuppance someday. People like her usually do. What you have to get cracking on now is a program of six great new cheers. Did I say great? I mean greater. Because if you're going to win now, you not only have to beat Garrison, you have to beat your own great cheers!"

"We can't do it," Nancy said, defeated. "Those were the best cheers we could write. We'll never come up with better ones. Especially not in less than a week!" She was clearly upset. Tears were beginning to well up in her eyes.

"Stop, Nancy," Ardith said gently, putting an arm around her shoulder. "You can't give up now." Then she turned back to the rest of them, and in a more severe tone said, "That goes for all of you. So you got a bad break. And I'll admit it's a particularly bad one. What are you going to do, just sit down and boohoo and give up? This is what sports are all about. When the going gets tough, the tough get going! And you kids are the toughest, best squad I've coached in my twenty years at Tarenton High. If anyone can pull this off and still come out on top, it's you! And I mean that!"

The room was silent for a while. Everyone was thinking through the problem in his or her own way.

I sure don't want to disappoint Ardith, Nancy thought, but six new cheers in six days is a tall order.

The best squad she'd had in twenty years? I didn't know that. It would be a shame for us to go down in defeat after how good we've become, Walt was thinking.

If I tell Claudia I've got to practice every night this week, I might as well kiss her good-bye, Pres realized.

The rest of the cheerleaders struggled with their own thoughts. Finally, Mary Ellen spoke up.

"It'll be gruesome, and if the rest of you decide to forget it, I can understand that. But the way I figure, we can do it."

"Then let's," Pres said, his voice also low and steady.

"Right on," Walt agreed.

"Count me in," Angie said.

"Me, too," Olivia added.

"Heyyyyy, Tarenton!" Nancy said in a low growly voice, a cheerleaders' cheer. "Let's knock 'em dead!"

The others smiled smiles that grew into large

grins. Ardith was infected by their spirit and started chuckling. They'd always been a team, a unit, but now they were conspirators in a secret mission, and the possibility of actually making it happen against these staggering odds was, in a strange way, exhilarating.

"We do have one rather largish problem," Ardith said. "If Vanessa has been able to steal our cheers up until now, who's to say she won't steal the new ones we come up with?"

"We could have someone hang out with her whenever we're practicing, to see that she doesn't get near the gym," Walt posed.

"No. That'd just make her suspicious," Nancy said. "Besides, she might have an accomplice who'd just go on stealing cheers while we were busy chaperoning Vanessa."

"We'll have to get a secret practice space," Mary Ellen said.

"But none of our houses — not even Pres's — really has any place large enough for us to do our jumps and tumbles and pyramids," Olivia pointed out.

"I think I can get the gym over at St. Paul's grade school," Angie volunteered. "I help the nuns with their Christmas pageant. I'm pretty sure Sister Jerome would give me the keys. Nothing happens over there at night, anyway. We could probably use it from eight to midnight."

"But won't Vanessa wonder what's going

on?" Pres wondered. "I mean, she'll see we're not practicing at school anymore."

"I'll put out the word tomorrow that I think you're ready for the competition and I'm giving you a few days off to rest up for it," Ardith said. "That ought to be enough to throw Vanessa off the scent."

"How are we going to get over to the gym without anyone seeing?" Walt asked. "Should we wear disguises?"

"What about if I pick everyone up in my moving van?" Pres suggested.

"My, my," Angie said. "Real spy stuff."

"I just hope it works," Nancy said.

"Well, we've just got to make it work." Mary Ellen's voice was trembling with emotion as she said this. "If it doesn't, I want us at least to be able to look back and say we gave it our absolute best."

Pres drove the moving van straight home from Ardith's when the meeting broke up. If he was going to be providing transportation all week to the secret practices, he couldn't leave the truck at Patrick's. He was just going to have to bring it home and let his father know about the new business, and take what came.

He went back to the kitchen where Marie the cook was cleaning up from dinner. Dinner! Instantly his memory came back to him. He had forgotten that Claudia was coming for dinner tonight. He glanced at the clock on the microwave. 8:37. Well, the meal was over, for sure. He'd missed it. He pulled a carton of milk out of the refrigerator and, under the silent glare of Marie, drank what was left without bothering with the formality of a glass. He tossed the empty carton in the trash basket, smiled at Marie, and sailed out of the kitchen to meet his fate.

He found it in the south parlor, where his parents were listening to Claudia play the piano. Mozart. He had to admit she was pretty talented. And smart. And beautiful. Plus she was exactly the kind of girl his parents wanted for him. He suspected he'd make all three of them happy by settling down with her.

Standing outside the parlor, he debated whether to run upstairs and change out of his grubby mover's clothes — torn jeans and an Army jacket. Sunday nights, the Tilfords dressed for dinner, and so he knew that beyond the parlor door he'd find his mother and Claudia in dresses and his father in a dinner jacket. Still, to find his own dress clothes and change would take another half hour. He decided that being scruffy was marginally better than being even later, and so he just went on in. Claudia stopped playing and all three of them looked up at him expectantly.

"Hi," he said. "Sorry I'm late. I got tied up."

"You look a little like you've been tied up,"

Claudia said, hiding her sarcasm from his parents behind teasing honey tones. "Tied up and thrown in a garbage can."

"You do look a little the worse for wear," Pres's father concurred from his big leather armchair in the corner. "Claudia was telling us at dinner all about your new enterprise."

Pres felt himself flush with rage. How could she just blab his secret to his parents? Whose side was she on, anyway?

"Looks like the work is a little hard on you," his mother said. He couldn't tell if she was being sarcastic, or what. He couldn't tell what was going on with any of them. Maybe they were just waiting for an apology.

"I'm sorry I missed dinner. I gather Claudia told you about the move. It was a little rougher than we expected. And a little longer. Anyway, I'm sorry I didn't call. I just got caught up in getting the job done. Then we had a shock. We found out that the squad is being sabotaged. Vanessa Barlow is conspiring with the enemy to do us in at the tri-state competition next weekend."

"Oh," Claudia said, putting a hand dramatically over her heart, "high tragedy."

Pres glared at her.

"It may seem like a joke to you, Claudia. But believe me, it's no joke to any of us on the squad. We've worked hard getting ready for this competition. But more than that, if we look bad,

146

we're letting down the whole school. Maybe back in Virginia, caring about your school just isn't cool, but up here it's one of the things that really matters."

When he stopped, he could see that Claudia was blushing. He looked at his parents. They seemed a little stunned by his outburst. At first he was afraid they were going to take Claudia's side and tell him he was out of line, but instead his father spoke to Claudia.

"I'm afraid Pres is right, my dear. Around here, being true to your school is a point of honor. Perhaps because you're away from your own hometown, you don't feel this allegiance as strongly, but I'm proud that Pres does."

Claudia looked desperately over at Mrs. Tilford, her last possible defender, but Pres's mother was off on her own nostalgic track.

"Oh, I remember the days when I was a Tarenton cheerleader. I remember one of the forwards on the Garrison basketball team asking me out for a date. I actually turned him down because I thought it would be a betrayal to our dear old Wolves."

"Uh, well," Claudia stammered, seeing she was outnumbered, "if you'll excuse me. I still tire rather easily — you know, since the operation. I'd really better be going."

"I'll see you to the door," Pres said. He had something he wanted to say to her, alone. When they got out onto the front porch, he whispered harshly, "Claudia, what made you tell my parents about the moving business? You knew I didn't want them to know so soon."

She waved him off with a dismissive hand.

"Oh Pres, don't be tiresome. Don't you realize how pitiful this little scheme of yours is? No one cares about it. You think your father's going to be all upset. Well, let me tell you, when I told him, he just smiled. He probably thinks it's a joke, too."

"I'll tell you what the joke is, Claudia," Pres said, really fuming now. "This relationship. You think you have me all figured out, and our future all planned. Well, why don't you factor this into your plan — I'm *through*. For all I care, you can get in that little Mercedes of yours and drive straight back to Virginia. Maybe you'll find some guy there who needs his life run for him. Me, I'd rather do it myself." And then, before he had to hear whatever she was about to say, Pres gently closed the door in her face.

Back in the house, Pres's father was waiting for him.

"So," he said, "I hear we've got two company presidents in the family now."

"Well, actually, I'm only a partner," Pres said shyly. "And so far it's a slightly smaller business than Tarenton Fabricators. And slightly less well-run, I'm afraid. I think we might have actually *lost* money on this first move, if you count in gas and depreciation on the truck."

"Oh, well, don't be discouraged yet," his father said, putting down his newspaper and leaning forward in his chair. "I don't think I ever told you this, but one of the first products Great-Grandfather Tilford manufactured at this factory was buggy whips. Unfortunately, he got production rolling just as Henry Ford was coming out with the Model A and people were trading in their horses for cars. It was not a terrific start."

Pres smiled. Whatever response he had expected from his dad, it wasn't this.

"You know," he went on, "I did a little moving myself. When I was in college."

"You did?"

"Oh yes. My father — unlike generous old me — didn't believe in allowances. So I had to find part-time jobs all through school. And I didn't have my own truck, either. I worked for a senior who did. I remember it as a lot of aches and pains. But I did learn a few things about the business. I could give you a few tips when you've got some time."

"Great," Pres said. "Oh. There's something else I guess I'd better mention, Dad. I'm not going to be seeing Claudia anymore." He was sure *this* would get a negative reaction. But once again his father turned up more surprising than a rabbit out of a hat.

"Oh. Well, I guess that means we can get back to eating regular food without all those strange sauces. Come on, then, I'd kind of like to see that truck of yours. And then we'll have to figure out how you can still keep a hand in this business, while you're away at Princeton."

Pres shook his head ruefully. He's still got Princeton on his brain. But by this time in this particular long day, Pres was way too tired to fight another battle in the continuing war.

CHAPTER

Usually Nancy looked forward to dinner-time with her parents. Especially since her father had started taking Chinese cooking lessons. Lots of nights, Nancy would help him out, chopping vegetables into tiny pieces and lining up spoons full of just the right measures of spices and oils, so that when he fired up the wok they'd be ready to go — tossing in everything at the right split second.

Monday, though, everything was out of whack. She came home from school exhausted from all that had happened Sunday. The work-out and the talk with Greg. Helping Pres and Patrick with their move. The emergency meeting at Ardith's. And then this afternoon, she'd had a killer test in chemistry. At moments like this, she looked forward to adulthood, when she hoped the pace would be a little easier.

When she got home, she headed straight for her room, turned on the radio, and hit the bed for a heavy-duty nap. She didn't wake up until her mother called up the stairs for her to come down to dinner.

There was no Chinese cooking tonight, no atmosphere of easy conversation, either. When Nancy came, bleary-eyed, into the kitchen, her mother was pulling some frozen entrees out of the microwave. Her father was watching the news on the little TV in the breakfast nook.

Since the scene over Greg on Friday, there had been a cloud of near-silence hanging over the three of them. Nancy wished she could break it, and was looking for a way into that conversation.

"What's this?" she asked her mother as she set a plate of something in front of her.

"I don't know. Something in cheese sauce."

"Can I have that other one?" Nancy asked. "The something in tomato sauce?"

This got a small laugh out of her mother.

"Am I a rotten mother, serving you this astronaut food?"

"Am I a rotten daughter," Nancy asked, "throwing a tantrum when you two were only trying to be part of my life?"

Her father looked over from the TV set, then clicked it off.

"Do you really understand that?" he asked her.

Nancy nodded, then said, "I think so. But I have to know for sure. If I told you I was in love with Greg and had considered all the difficulties and still wanted to go on with him, would you really accept that decision?"

"Of course," her mother said. "We've put in seventeen years encouraging you to become an independent person. If we've succeeded, you're sometimes going to make choices we don't understand right off the bat. We just want you to talk to us so we *can* understand."

"I think I got on my high horse before. I thought you were attacking Greg, and I felt like I had to defend him. Now he and I've decided to just be friends, so I guess the whole argument is a moot point, anyway."

"It's not, though," her father said, looking down at his entree as if he'd seen it move. "The argument was never really about Greg. It was about how we're going to fine tune our relationship with you now that you're becoming an adult."

"Well, blowing up was not very adult of me," Nancy said.

"Oh, I don't know," her father mused. "I've blown up a few times since I've been an adult. What about you, Eleanor?" he asked Nancy's mother.

"What about me? Well, I'm thinking about

fixing a fast salad to go with this stuff. Maybe I can fake it into looking like a real meal. Nance, when are you sneaking out into the dark of night for the high-espionage practice?" One of the things Nancy loved best about her folks was that once an argument with them was over, it was over.

The practice surprised everyone by being a lot more fun than regular workouts. Part of it was the secret-mission atmosphere. Another part was the high energy level. Putting together an entire new program at the eleventh hour like this was a lot like being in the final minutes of a really close game. It just brought out the best — and most — in everyone.

Angie had already written a new cheer.

"I probably flunked my history quiz on account of this, so I hope you all appreciate it," she said. Mary Ellen grabbed the cheer out of her hand and the rest of them started working out a formation for it.

Even though it was late, and the night was cool and there was no heat on in the little grade school gym, no one complained about being too tired or too cold. None of them thought about their individual problems or worries. For tonight and the rest of the week, they weren't Mary Ellen and Angie and Pres and Walt and Olivia and Nancy. They were the Tarenton Varsity Cheerleading Squad. Best in the region.

* * *

Around ten that night, Vanessa Barlow was driving Betty Sims home after another meeting at the Taco Taco. Betty was holding onto a copy of the cheer program Ardith had printed out that day.

"Well, that about does it, I think," Vanessa said. "Now you've got nearly a week to perfect these."

"Are you going to come to the competition?" Betty asked.

"Are you kidding?" Vanessa said with a sneering grin. "And see those sweet Tarenton cheerleaders fall flat on their pretty faces? I wouldn't miss it for the world!"

A few blocks from Betty's house, they passed St. Paul's school.

"Hmmm. Look at that," Vanessa mused idly. "Ten o'clock and all the lights are still on. Those little tykes are sure up way past their bedtime."

CHAPTER

Friday night on the bus to Summerville, Angie and Mary Ellen were curled up in their favorite side-by-side seats in the back, Angie's radio propped on the armrest between them, playing low. On the way to and from games was some of their best talking time. Only tonight they weren't on their way to a game. The bus was mostly empty since there wasn't a team aboard — just the six cheerleaders, Mrs. Engborg, and Patrick, who was along to photograph the competition for the school paper and yearbook.

As the bus cruised through the night along the straight shot of interstate, the atmosphere inside was unusually subdued. The squad was in a pensive mood, looking back on all the work of the past week, and forward, to the competition tomorrow. They had practiced as hard as they could, and then harder. The challenge of beating Garrison, and all the other squads who would come, *and* the desire to foil Vanessa, had supercharged them into a huge burst of creative activity.

"You know," Angie said in a low voice to Mary Ellen, "this may sound crazy, but I think the new program is better than our original one."

"Oh, I think you're right. Our hello cheer is super. Our home cheer is truly awesome. The International Cheerleading Foundation cheer — well, that's the same for everyone; we can only go for execution on that. And our finals cheer — if we make it that far — ought to knock everyone's socks off. Somebody might have as good a program, but nobody's going to have a better one. And Garrison's only got our *old* program, so I don't think we have to worry too much about our archrivals."

"But I hear Elmwood has a fabulous squad. Walt saw them when he was on that trip with his parents. He says they're like a cheerleading machine."

"Well," Mary Ellen said, yawning, "I'll have to worry about Elmwood tomorrow. I'm just too tired tonight." But she wasn't about to get any sleep in the near future.

When they got to the Thrifty Inn outside Summerville, Mrs. Engborg registered them and passed out the room keys.

"You girls will be in 219, boys in 221. I'll be in between in 220, trying to get a decent night's sleep, and I trust you'll all be doing the same."

Ardith was whistling in the wind. She knew that, tired as the squad was, seven teenagers away from home for the night were not about to put on their sleeping caps, snuff out the candle, and go to bed.

The guys dumped their stuff and soon found the game room downstairs, which was full of cheerleaders from other squads around the tri-state region. The girls stayed in their room, redoing each other's makeup in front of the huge lit-up vanity mirror. Angie had brought along a hair-streaking kit and they all gave each other matching streaks coming off their left temples. Because their natural hair colors were so different, the streaks too were wildly different. Mary Ellen's was nearly white, Nancy's an orangy color from outer space. When they were done and surveying the results in the mirror, they loved the little flash of unity the streaks would give them tomorrow. They also decided they'd dye them back to normal as soon as they got home. Except Olivia.

"I really like mine," she said. "Besides, I think my mother is going to hate it. Which is a big plus in its favor."

Pres and Patrick and Walt came by with sodas and chips from the machines, and partying on their minds. They groaned when they saw the streaks, then groaned harder when the girls pushed the door shut on them.

"Ardith would kill us if she found you guys in here," said Mary Ellen, speaking for all of them.

The guys reluctantly went back to their room — Walt making a last try by saying he wanted his own streak — and the girls got in bed. They started watching *Casablanca* on the late movie, but all four of them were asleep long before Humphrey Bogart said good-bye to Ingrid Bergman at the airport.

Angie woke up in the middle of the night, shut off the TV, which was just flecks by now, got back into bed, and woke up Mary Ellen.

"Are we going to win?" she asked. This short night of fooling around was the first time in a week that she'd forgotten the competition for even a moment. Now worry was swooping over her again.

"Yes, we'll win," Mary Ellen said seriously, then turned over and both of them went back to sleep.

The next thing any of them knew it was early Saturday morning and Ardith was pounding on their door.

"Come on. Down to the coffee shop in half an hour! It's time to get up and go show everyone what Tarenton's got up its sleeve!"

The Tri-State High School Cheerleading Competition was held in the field house of Templeton

College. Seventy-eight squads from around the region had come in for it. Each squad would have five minutes to perform three cheers: a hello cheer, a home cheer, and a prescribed International Cheerleading Foundation cheer. The ten finalists would compete with a special fourth cheer.

There were hundreds of people in the stands, rooting for the various squads. The floor was bustling with coaches and advisers and packs and packs of cheerleaders, fully dressed in their school colors. The event was already a pandemonium of color and noise.

Ardith drew the Tarenton squad aside and showed them a copy of the evaluation sheet the judges would be using.

"Here are the judging criteria," she said. "You'll be given points for spirit, audience appeal, personality projection, squad unity, voice, appearance, and confidence. Cheers will be scored on creativity and originality, and on skill of execution. They'll be looking at your jumps, gymnastics, partner stunts, and pyramids."

"How are we going to keep all that in mind at the same time?!" Olivia wailed.

"Don't worry about everything at once," Ardith said. "Just go for it with your strong points, while trying to boost your weak areas. For you, Livvy, that's eye contact. I want to see you boring holes through those judges with your cheery gaze. The rest of you, you know where you need to focus. The only other thing I want to say is that I've been watching some of the other squads working out and I think you've got a good chance here."

The competition began at ten sharp. The five judges sat at a long table, marking evaluation sheets as each squad came up for its turn. The Tarenton cheerleaders waited and watched and waited some more, feeling their nerves getting frayed.

Garrison came up a little past one in the afternoon. Predictably, they ran through every one of Tarenton's original cheers. Afterward they gleefully rushed off the floor, slapping each other's hands in anticipated victory. Betty Sims left the pack and ran over and gave a big hug of thanks to Vanessa, who was waiting by an exit, in the shadow of the stands.

"It makes me crazy to watch," Angie whispered to Mary Ellen. "You know, even through this whole week, I kept hoping we were wrong, that Vanessa was just helping Betty with her geometry at Taco Taco that night, that when Garrison got out on the floor, they'd do a program of cheers we'd never seen before. But it's true, isn't it? And there's Vanessa, the traitor. Do you think anyone would mind if I went over and just strangled her?"

"Forget it," Mary Ellen said, draping a consoling arm across Angie's shoulder. "We've got a better routine than the one she gave them. Look at it this way. She may have actually done us a favor. Her little stunt forced us to push harder than we had been on our own. Which gives us a better chance of winning. So don't think about her. Besides, there are more interesting people in the stands at the moment than Vanessa Barlow."

"Huh?" Angie said, bewildered.

"Why don't you look just above the exit sign in Section 12," Mary Ellen said cryptically, then walked off to talk with Patrick.

Angie scanned the bleachers until she found the sign for Section 12. Then she found the exit and looked above it. What she saw there was a bunch of people she didn't know and one she did. Chris Page. Her heart thumped inside her chest. Before, she had lots of reasons to put her all into her performance today, Now, though, she had the best one yet. She was going to make it a poem for him.

A little before three, Mrs. Engborg rushed over and told the squad they were now third down the list. So far, they thought they had most of the competition beat. The only squads they were worried about were the "machine" from Elmwood, which had just been up and looked very good, and Garrison because of their execution, which had been flawless.

As they moved up, two away from their turn,

then next in line, their tension grew. Nancy thought she'd jump out of her skin if they didn't get out on the floor soon. Walt was sweating. Pres was wringing his hands, which he only did when he was in his highest state of nervousness. Luckily for all of them, just as they were going out onto the floor, the spell of anxiety was broken in the most amazing and unexpected way. Suddenly there arose from the stands a booming chorus of the world's oldest, corniest cheer:

> "Two-four-six-eight,
> Who do we appreciate?
> Tarenton — yea!"

They all looked up and laughed. There were the entire basketball and football teams of Tarenton High, turning the tables — cheering their cheerleaders. With this kind of support, how could they be anything but great?

They ran through their program in synchronized perfection. They were the best they'd ever been. Pres didn't collapse under his end of the pyramid. Nancy didn't miss her leap up onto Walt's shoulders. Olivia remembered to smile and make eye contact so she didn't look like a robot. Every one of them was in absolutely peak form.

When they tumbled out of the final pyramid, they heard a roar of applause, much more than could be attributed to the Tarenton contingent, even with all those football and basketball players clapping as hard as they could. This meant the crowd in general liked them. Well, not the entire crowd.

Pres was the first to check out the reaction from Garrison. Every one of their cheerleaders was standing there, glaring in furious disbelief.

"Oh, I feel so sorry for them," he said to Walt. "Their little scheme's gone up in smoke. And there goes Betty Sims in a big hurry. Do you think she's looking for her old pal Vanessa?"

Walt chuckled and said, "I'd like to be a fly on the wall when she catches up with her."

Tarenton made it into the finals, but Garrison did, too. So did Elmwood. The other seven finalists all had fatal flaws; they weren't real contenders. The real final round would be between these three.

And for this round, Garrison knew they had no edge on Tarenton. And they had no idea how good Tarenton's final cheer would be. Maybe it was this uncertainty that threw them off. Maybe it was Betty's last-minute return from her search for Vanessa. Whatever the case, Garrison messed up on two of the three synchronized jumps in their routine. At this stage, with everything riding on nuances of perfection, everyone knew this was probably enough to put them out of the running. And then their already glum expressions turned to looks of despair as they watched the Tarenton squad come out onto the floor and pound out the best cheer they'd ever done.

The Tarenton High cheerleaders tumbled out onto the floor, into a pyramid from which they began chanting:

> "Red, white!
> Red, white!
> Fight, fight!
> S-P-I-R-I-T!
> Spirit! Spirit!
> We've got to cheer it!
> So let's hear it!
> Go Tarenton! Yea!!"

Coming out of the pyramid, Olivia and Angie sprung off a mini-trampoline, onto the shoulders of Walt and Pres, while Mary Ellen and Nancy did triple cartwheels into suicide jumps.

The crowd went wild. Still, it was hard to tell who had won. Elmwood had made its final entry a breakdance routine that was impressive in a trendy sort of way. As they waited for the judges' decision, the Tarenton cheerleaders speculated on the outcome.

"Elmwood'll get it," Olivia said dejectedly. "Why didn't we think of putting together something like that?"

"Don't worry," Walt said, giving her a quick kiss. "This panel of judges has been going for the traditional right down the line. They're not going to change now."

But in spite of Walt's brave words, he looked as nervous as the rest of the squad, when the head judge picked up the microphone.

Standing before the hundreds of people in the field house, he announced, "The winner of this year's Tri-State High School Cheerleading competition is Tarenton High."

The entire squad went crazy. Walt hugged Olivia. Pres kissed Nancy and then Mary Ellen and then Angie. And then they all hugged Mrs. Engborg, who looked completely stunned. Then Chris Page was there swooping Angie up in his arms. Then Patrick gave up trying to take pictures and let Mary Ellen swoop *him* up. And then the Tarenton contingent descended from the stands and carried the squad off the floor and out of the field house on their shoulders.

As they were being floated out on this sea of shoulders, Nancy looked over to see two more surprise fans: Greg Connors in his wheelchair, being pushed along by Eric Campbell. It was Eric who caught Nancy's hand and pulled her down to his face level and kissed her. Maybe it was a kiss that came out of the excitement of the moment. Nancy couldn't be sure. She couldn't even think about it in the midst of all this. But she knew she would later. Eric Campbell. Hmmm.

Out in the parking lot, the team members set

the cheerleaders down. The six of them caught their breath and looked at each other and couldn't stop smiling. Not then. Not on the bus home. Not into the night as they each lay in their own beds, drifting into dream-filled sleep.

The squad is together but in terrible trouble . . . the most serious they have ever faced. Read Cheerleaders #17, Taking Risks.

Join the Team!

They're talented. They're fabulous-looking. They're winners! And they've got what you want! **Don't miss any of these exciting CHEERLEADERS books!**

Watch for these titles! $2.25 each

Books chosen with you in mind from

—Pass the word.

Living...loving...growing.
That's what **POINT** books are all about!
They're books you'll love reading and
will want to tell your friends about.

Don't miss these other exciting **Point** titles!

NEW POINT TITLES! $2.25 each

- ☐ QI 33306-2   **The Karate Kid** B.B. Hiller
- ☐ QI 31987-6   **When We First Met** Norma Fox Mazer
- ☐ QI 32512-4   **Just the Two of Us** Hila Colman
- ☐ QI 32338-5   **If This Is Love, I'll Take Spaghetti** Ellen Conford
- ☐ QI 32728-3   **Hello...Wrong Number** Marilyn Sachs
- ☐ QI 33216-3   **Love Always, Blue** Mary Pope Osborne
- ☐ QI 33116-7   **The Ghosts of Departure Point** Eve Bunting
- ☐ QI 33195-7   **How Do You Lose Those Ninth Grade Blues?** Barthe DeClements
- ☐ QI 33550-2   **Charles in Charge** Elizabeth Faucher
- ☐ QI 32306-7   **Take It Easy** Steven Kroll
- ☐ QI 33409-3   **Slumber Party** Christopher Pike

📚 **Scholastic Inc.**
   P.O. Box 7502, 2932 East McCarty Street, Jefferson City, MO 65102

Please send me the books I have checked above. I am enclosing
$_____ (please add $1.00 to cover shipping and handling). Send
check or money order—no cash or C.O.D.'s please.

Name_____

Address_____

City_____State/Zip_____
POI851   Please allow four to six weeks for delivery.